HOUSE without LIES

RACHEL BRANTON

WHITE
STAR
PRESS

This is a work of fiction, and the views expressed herein are the sole responsibility of the author. Likewise, certain characters, places, and incidents are the product of the author's imagination, and any resemblance to actual persons, living or dead, or actual events or locales, is entirely coincidental.

House Without Lies (Lily's House Book 1)

Published by White Star Press
P.O. Box 353
American Fork, Utah 84003

Printed in the United States of America
ISBN: 978-1-939203-69-4
Year of first printing: 2016

Thanks to my husband and family for letting me disappear into my office for hours at a time. Also thanks to my great editors, Cátia, Maria, and Jenn, for their sharp eyes and great suggestions that allowed me to make this story better than I could on my own.

1

I looked both ways as I headed into the alley behind the store, not because I was embarrassed, but because I didn't want to get Payden in trouble for slipping out to meet me there. The boy was going to a lot of effort to help me, and my runaway girls always needed the food he donated. Unfortunately, I didn't have my car today, and I was already balancing two bags of groceries I'd purchased when I'd gone inside the store to signal Payden that I was here. So whatever he had for us would make my walk home that much more difficult.

He was already outside in the alley, waiting at the back door by the green Dumpster, his round, heavily-freckled face grinning as always. The roundness made him look younger than his seventeen years, and rather innocent.

"Hey, Lily," he greeted me, shifting the large box in his arms so he could give a friendly wave. His blue apron was splashed with something that had turned it purple, and the sagging material made him look chubby. He puffed a breath upward to blow away the straight-cut brown hair that hung like a shield over his brown eyes.

"Hey, Payden." I hooked the grocery bags over my wrists and pushed them toward my elbows, freeing up my hands so I could take the box from him. "Thank you so much."

"Got bread, bagels, muffins, and cookies today. Should last if you freeze them."

I could also see dented cans, a few vegetables that would make a fabulous soup, and a gallon of expiring milk. "This is great. Are you sure you won't get into trouble? That other clerk in there was looking at me kind of strange."

He shrugged. "Makes no sense to throw it in the trash if you're right here." He laughed. "I can always say you wrestled me for it." His smile dimmed slightly, and he waited only a second to add, "How is she?"

"Elsie's doing great. Really. The bruising is almost gone. I'll try to bring her next time, if she'll come."

His smile returned. "Then she didn't run away again."

"Nope. She still thinks whoever she's running from is looking for her, but no one's tracked her down yet. Plus, she's worried child services will find her and make her go back."

He folded his arms, looking for all the world as if he wanted to do battle for her. The expression sat oddly on his young face. "They probably would. She's better off with you."

If going back to her family or staying with me were the only options, I was the better choice—one glance at the picture I'd taken of Elsie after finding her in this very alley three weeks ago was proof of that.

I'd heard Elsie's pitiful sobs from the main street and

hurried to find her collapsed on the ground near the Dumpster, which she'd apparently been trying to open to find food. Her numerous cuts were old, but not healing, and a deep black and green bruise mottled most of her feverish face. When I'd lifted Elsie up, her battered ribs showed through a gaping rip in her shirt.

That's when Payden had found us and given me that first box of expired groceries. He was a kindred spirit. Too bad he wasn't five years older. But then, even men my age seemed too young these days. All they cared about was partying, scraping by in their university courses, and more partying.

"Thanks again." I didn't tell him Elsie hadn't gone outside at all since last week when our neighbor on the second floor had seen her in the stairwell and questioned her about where she lived. Knowing would only make Payden feel bad, and it wasn't something he could change.

"You're welcome." He turned to go inside but hesitated at the door. "Hey, you should really talk to my cousin. I told you he's working at a place here in Phoenix that helps troubled kids. Teen Remake, or something. He's got connections, you know? He's dropping some stuff off for me soon. If you wait just a minute, I could introduce you."

"I don't think so. I can't betray Elsie's trust. She's been through enough." I could probably be charged for harboring a minor, and if my own family found out, I suspected they would come down on the side of the law. Well, all but my sister, Tessa, who had helped me out more than once in the past few months. Anyway, it wasn't likely Payden's cousin could do anything more than I could about helping Elsie.

"Think about it," Payden urged.

"I will."

I trudged up the alley, tripping once on an old tire someone had left in the way but catching myself before I fell. Lugging the groceries all the way back to my apartment on foot wasn't something I was looking forward to. Saffron, the oldest of the runaways who lived with me, had chosen a rotten day to borrow my car, but her job interview this morning had to come first.

Cars honked and whizzed past as I reached the main street. Downtown Phoenix was never quiet, it seemed, and today was particularly busy. The air already felt hot and dry on my face.

"Lily!"

I turned at the voice and saw Payden, but this time he stood in the front doorway of the small grocery store. A man I'd never seen before was with him, and I hoped Payden wasn't in trouble for helping me. Would they take back the groceries?

As I watched, the man pushed past Payden and stepped out onto the wide sidewalk. My heart stopped. He was a good two heads taller than Payden and handsome enough that I remembered I wasn't wearing makeup, and that my messy ponytail had to be more mess than ponytail.

"My cousin's going to help you get those to your car," Payden said, nodding encouragingly. He jerked his head to the side, as if listening to someone from behind him. "Gotta go."

The relief inside me that Payden wasn't in trouble was canceled out by the amused smile on the man's face.

Without introducing himself, he reached for the box. "So, where's your car?"

His black hair was short except on top in the front, where it partially waved, arching up and then down in a way that I found compelling. His eyes, also dark, spoke of something exotic. Up close, not even one freckle marred his face, but there was a bit of a five o'clock shadow, as if he'd missed shaving today.

This was Payden's cousin? If I'd known he was this attractive, I might have hit him up for help a long time ago.

I kept hold of the box. "I didn't bring it. Sorry. But it's okay. I don't need help."

"I don't mind walking to your place. Where do you live?" He tugged again gently on the box, his bronzed arms brushing mine. I couldn't tell if his skin color came from heredity or the sun.

"Are you sure you're Payden's cousin? Because you don't look like him."

He laughed, a sound that warmed me clear through to my stomach. "People say that a lot. But we are cousins— our mothers are sisters. I just have a bit more variety in my gene pool from my dad's side."

Definitely a combination that was working for him. "Well, I'm used to carrying the boxes Payden gives me. But thank you."

He lifted the box from my arms anyway. "What kind of gentleman would I be if I didn't walk you home?"

"Maybe you just want to know where I live."

Again the laugh. "Actually, I do want to know. That way I'll know where to pick you up when we go out."

When we go out? A thousand butterflies took flight in my stomach. "Who said I'm going out with you?"

He gave me a slow grin that only increased my heartbeat. "You'll come around. Now where are we going?"

All at once, I wanted to let him help. I'd been doing this alone for so long, and I couldn't recall when I'd last been on a date—or flirted with a guy. Certainly not in the past six months.

"Okay," I said. Letting this gorgeous stranger carry a box ten blocks wasn't going to hurt either of us. "But keep up. I have stuff to do. And my roommates are waiting for me."

"Roommates, huh?"

"I have a few."

Six to be exact. Girls living on the street seemed to have some kind of internal radar where I was concerned. They appeared in my vicinity, obviously in need, and I couldn't help taking them home. Elsie, our newest addition, had been the last straw for my old roommates, but I was still trying to see getting kicked out of their apartment as a good thing. My new place was a dump, but at least the girls didn't have to hide in my room or sneak in only at night to sleep. And there were no complaints about them stealing food.

"So, have you lived here long?" I asked him.

"Five years. I came for school, but I love it here and I don't think I'll ever leave. I'm from Tucson originally. You?"

"Flagstaff. I've been here for most of three years. It's a nice place—well, not downtown so much but the city in general." I wouldn't tell him what I liked best was being away from Flagstaff and my parents. "Is your whole family here?"

"Just Payden and his mom. His dad died a few years back. That's one of the reasons I moved here, to help them out. My family's still in Tucson. I have three brothers and two sisters."

"That many?"

He laughed again, and it made me smile just to hear it. "Yeah. You have any?"

"One sister. She's here, too. Across town." Tessa didn't know I'd moved, and I was a little embarrassed to tell her. She'd warned me it would happen, but how could I have left Elsie in the street?

No, Tessa would understand, and she'd volunteer to help, if I needed her. She managed the swing shift at Crawford Cereals, our dad's factory, so our hours overlapped, and it would be easy enough to pull her aside and tell her there. If my parents got wind of it, however, there would be repercussions. They'd wanted me to come home after the college semester ended and, when I'd stayed, had barely let me continue my part-time job at the factory.

They didn't know about the girls, or that I was their only support. Now that school was out, I was thinking about finding a second job. The twenty hours at the factory weren't cutting it, and I'd already used much of my savings account.

Beside me, Payden's cousin slowed. "Hey, where'd you go?"

I refocused on him. "Sorry. Just thinking about something I have to do later." Then before he could probe further, I said, "I don't even know your name. But I can keep calling you Payden's cousin, if you want."

"If I tell you, will you go out with me?"

"If you don't tell me, I won't go out with you."

"That's not exactly a yes."

"Nope." I gave him a slow grin.

"Okay, my name is Mario Perez."

An unexpected laugh burst through me. He didn't look like a Mario Perez. "Mario? You mean like the game?"

"No way, you play video games?"

"Of course I play video games." Games were one way to connect with the girls, so I learned to play, and sometimes I even enjoyed it.

"Well, that's really my name. I'm named after my grandfather who came from Spain."

Europe. So that explained the olive skin and exotic features. "You don't look like a Mario." I studied him more closely. In the video game world, Mario was short and, well, a cartoon.

"My middle name is Jameson," he offered. "But only my mom and my aunt call me that. Everyone else calls me Mario."

"Okay. I'm sure there's a story behind that."

He grinned, and once more that strange heat curled through my belly. If he asked me to go out again, I was definitely saying yes.

"My mother named me, but she changed her mind about calling me Mario after the birth certificate was filed and began using my middle name instead. But my dad said that if Jameson was the name she'd wanted, she should have put it first." He laughed. "It's become a friendly little tug-of-war between them. Basically, I've learned to answer to just about anything."

"Sounds fun," I lied. Not if their wars were anything like the ones my parents waged. Those always sent both Tessa and me running for cover. "You do look more like a Jameson to me. But maybe I'd better pick something safer. Like MJ." I regretted the words the minute they escaped my lips because MJ didn't fit him at all.

His grin grew wider. "A nickname. Does that mean you'll go out with me?"

I was prevented from responding as a motorcycle roared by, and when I could hear again, the moment had passed. I jerked my head toward the four-story apartment complex. "That's where I live. I can take it from here."

"I don't mind walking you to your door."

As long as it was only to the door. With seven of us crammed into the one-bedroom apartment, I had no idea what to expect of the inside. I'd given the girls chores, but this early most of them would still be in bed, except Saffron, who was at her job interview, and the two sisters I had guardianship over, who were in school.

"It's on the fourth floor," I warned, "and there's no elevator."

"Of course there isn't."

He'd obviously taken in the peeling paint, the planter boxes filled with weeds, and the litter on the ground. But it was cheap, and the owners didn't mind the girls "visiting" me. Or at least as long as we didn't make too much noise or come in large groups around the other tenants. Mostly, the place was so run down that they were eager to accept just about anyone.

I hurried up the four flights of open stairs, and Jameson wasn't puffing hard as he kept up. That was a good sign. But the closer we got to my apartment, the more worried I became. I had a lot to hide, and maybe thinking I could date like a normal person was crazy.

Why did Jameson have to be so incredibly yummy?

He followed me down the inner corridor, where I paused in front of my door. "This is it," I announced.

He waited expectantly, but there was no way he was carrying that box inside, not when I could guess what was waiting. And I'd have little time to clean before I rushed to my four-hour shift at the factory this afternoon.

A tiny tendril of moisture curled down from Jameson's temple, and even that was sexy. His dark eyes met mine. "So, Lily, will you go out with me? Payden says you're my type."

The door in front of us whooshed open, revealing Halla, a sixteen-year-old with blond hair so short she reminded me of a marine. She also had a penchant for army camouflage and tank tops, which added to the impression. Halla was tiny, though, mostly from malnutrition, so her tough act didn't carry much weight, but we were working on getting her what she needed.

"Elsie's on the roof again!" Halla blurted excitedly. "She was just sitting out there on the balcony and then bang, up she went."

"Oh, no." I darted a worried glance at Jameson. Forget about yummy or dating; I wished he'd leave.

Another face appeared behind Halla. This time a tall black girl who was only fourteen but looked at least eighteen. Ruth had shoulder-length hair that I usually plaited in tiny, meticulous braids, although today it was a frizzy mess under a baseball cap. She was model gorgeous, but she always covered her lithe figure in too-large clothes to hide any trace of femininity. After what she'd been through, I didn't blame her.

"I told you we shouldn't let anyone up there, even with you," Ruth said. "Elsie thinks none of the rules apply to her."

She had it wrong. I was pretty sure I knew what had spooked Elsie. I pushed a sack at each girl and reached for the box. "Sorry," I told Jameson. "Gotta go."

His eyes went from me to the girls and back. "You need some help?"

"No. Elsie will only get hurt if she thinks you're here for her."

"Here for her? Why, what's she done?" A crease marred his forehead.

Great. I'd known his following me home like a Boy Scout was a bad idea. I yanked the box from his unwilling arms and shoved it at Ruth. "Nothing. Goodbye, Jameson. And thanks." I pushed past the girls and entered the apartment, leaving Ruth to get rid of him. She was a protective mother hen, and she'd know his presence here was dangerous.

"So no nickname?" he called after me.

I didn't answer. What had I been thinking? Any kind of a romantic relationship now was completely out of the question. I had to think of Elsie and the other girls. Two of them had already tried to kill themselves.

The balcony ran the length of our apartment, which meant the living room and the bedroom, but the ladder that led to the fire escape and up onto the roof was located on the living room side. I stepped over blankets and backpacks and other strewn belongings on my way across the tiny living room, where a lump told me one of the girls was still sleeping. I kept walking a few paces until it dawned on me that I had no idea who the lump might be. Elsie was on the roof, Saffron at her interview, Ruth and Halla were here, and the other two were in school. I shook my head. I'd have to deal with whoever it was later.

It was my fault Elsie was on the roof. One night I'd climbed up in search of privacy, and when a couple of the girls had come looking for me, I'd answered their calls. Before long, all of us were up there.

Now it had become almost a nightly ritual for which-ever girls were home, a place where we could talk in the dark with only the stars as witnesses. I'd learned more about their lives there than anywhere else. Except for Elsie, who never talked but would sometimes reach out and clutch my hand.

The rules were that no one could go up without me because while the roof was large and barely slanted, we were on the fourth floor and some of the girls were still recovering from substance abuse. A couple of them also had quick tempers or were big jokers and as of yet didn't understand things like gravity and permanent consequences.

I jumped on the chair and climbed the ladder, easing over the edge on my hands and knees for a few feet until I reached the almost flat part and could walk upright. Elsie wasn't in plain view, but I found her hiding behind several air conditioning units that were already working overtime. Her forehead was pressed to her bare knees, and her long hair splayed outward in a wild, tangled mess, looking dark against her pale skin.

"Hey," I said, sliding into the empty space next to her.

She looked past me before replying, her brown eyes deep and unrevealing. "Is he looking for me?" The throaty words were full of dread.

"Oh, honey. No. Never."

She gave a little sob and pushed into my arms. At twelve, she was the youngest of the girls, and with how beaten she'd been when she arrived, the rest of us felt protective toward her—a good thing, or Halla and Ruth wouldn't have even noticed she was on the roof.

"Who is he?" she said after a few moments.

"Payden's cousin. He helped me bring home some groceries."

The remaining tautness in her body eased. "Good."

"Is there something you're not telling me?"

Elsie pulled away and nodded. "Yesterday when everyone was gone, I was on the balcony and I saw a little cat out in the parking lot. I thought I'd just go down to pet him for a minute and see if he was hungry, but that guy downstairs saw me and followed me, so I ran around the block and snuck back in." Elsie's teeth clamped down on her lips. "It was like he knew something and wanted to ask me more questions." Tears filled her eyes, spilling over when she blinked. "I won't go back. I'd jump off this roof before I'd go back."

Terror clutched at my chest. "No, Elsie. That's not going to happen. We'll find a way. Once I graduate, it'll be different. You'll see."

Changing my major twice now seemed ridiculous. The nursing classes had come in handy when Elsie arrived, but I should have pushed on with the business degree my parents had wanted—or at the very least avoided the year deviation into psychology. I could have finished by now, and have a good job cutting paychecks and balancing books at Crawford Cereals, even if it was a job I knew I'd detest. At this rate, I'd be an old woman before I graduated and had a job with enough money to do my dream work of helping lost girls.

The terrible irony was that I had money—a lot of money—just out of reach. An inheritance left to me by my grandfather, who'd founded Crawford Cereals: a half million dollars and monthly payments thereafter. But I had to be twenty-five and married, or thirty if I was still single, to access the funds. My parents had means, but convincing them would be impossible.

I needed to find a way to become legitimate, so the girls could get health and dental coverage and other benefits, but I didn't know where to begin. Risking that Elsie or any of the others might be sent back to the horrible situations they'd run from was not an option. At least with me, they didn't have to prostitute themselves or endure abuse by the very people who were supposed to protect them.

"Thanks, Lily."

At Elsie's soft words, the fear in my heart melted. I would make it work. Somehow.

Until I did, gorgeous and witty guys like Jameson were a distraction I didn't need.

After another twenty minutes, Elsie was calm enough to climb down from the roof. Heat gathered on the tile, so we were drenched in sweat, and all my thoughts were on how fast I could get into a cool shower and then to work. Had Saffron returned with my car? If she hadn't, I'd need to call my sister for a ride.

What I didn't expect to see was Jameson sitting on our ripped-up couch from Goodwill with girls perched on either end, huge slices of pizza in their hands.

"Wook!" Ruth said, her mouth crammed full. "Pipa."

"Pizza? At"—I reached into the pocket of my jeans to check my phone—"ten in the morning. Seriously?"

The girls laughed, but Jameson had the grace to look embarrassed. "We got hungry waiting for you," he said. "Ruth mentioned you had to go to work, and she wanted to make sure you got food, so I suggested pizza." Of course Ruth had been thinking of me.

"It was a good idea." Halla finished her piece and reached for another.

Jameson had no idea what he'd gotten himself into because these two and Elsie would probably eat the entire pizza inside ten minutes. Good thing he'd ordered a large.

I was more worried about why he was still here.

"You want one?" Jameson leaned forward and offered the box to Elsie. She didn't smile, but she took a piece after Ruth nodded encouragingly.

"You?" Jameson moved the box toward me. He held my gaze, his smile tentative. I became all too aware of my sweat-drenched body and my messy hair.

"Maybe in a minute. I need to shower." What I really needed was for him to get out of here. I couldn't exactly leave a man I didn't know with my underage girls, even if he was Payden's cousin.

I took a step forward—and my foot landed on the lump I'd seen earlier.

"Umph!" groaned the figure.

Trying to keep my balance, I whipped my other foot forward, but I was already falling. Jameson obligingly leapt up, grabbing me with his free arm, and we tumbled to the couch together.

"Beans!" I muttered. I didn't allow cursing in the apartment, and that included me, so some days we heard more about beans than we did most any other word. Jameson laughed and released me.

Seated on the couch, I reached for the blanket and pulled it off to reveal my best friend, Makayla Greyson. "Makay! When did you get here?"

She sat up, her single dark braid hanging over her shoulder. She rubbed her eyes with one hand, the other still protectively touching the small figure of a sleeping child. "Sorry. My place got too rowdy last night. I couldn't keep Nate there."

I wasn't surprised. Makay's roommates were so awful that the landlord had threatened to evict them five times in the past two weeks since she'd found me this place. "Well, that's why I gave you a key," I said. With Makay's stepmother descending into substance abuse, Makay had taken over the primary care of her little brother, and she didn't have a lot of options. "How's Nate?" I added.

Makay smiled, revealing a slight gap between her two front teeth. "Better than me—he sleeps like a rock." She sniffed. "Is that pizza?"

Jameson leaned over me and offered her the box. I could smell his cologne, and that meant he could probably smell me. I stifled a groan as I pushed myself out from under his arm and stood. "Sorry for stepping on you."

"Believe me, I've had worse," Makay said. "Anyway, I needed to wake up. I have to work. Can any of you watch Nate today? I can't pay, but I've got some great coupons for some free stuff I'm going to pick up on the way home. I'll share it all."

Ruth reached for the toddler. "You kidding? I'd love to. He's such an angel. You don't have to buy me nothing."

"Thank you, but I will anyway." Makay looked at me. "Can I talk to you for a minute?"

"Sure."

Feeling eyes on my face, I glanced over at Jameson. His expression was just the slightest bit confused, and I had to give him points for that. Most people would be really over-the-top crazy with all the chaos here.

"Go ahead," he said. "I can wait until you need to go. I'll walk you down. Got some pizza to finish."

Fine, he could eat his stinking pizza and then get out of my life. Because even if he wasn't over-the-top crazy, he was still a complication I obviously couldn't afford. I had to put these girls first. End of story. "I won't be long."

Makay and I went to the bedroom together, where the double mattress I'd bought at a yard sale rested on the floor near our two single Walmart-special, fold-out chair mattresses, leaving an open path around the outer edges. Blankets, pillows, backpacks, clothing, and other belongings lay heaped on top of the mattresses. I made the girls organize it every day, but it was hard to keep it clean with four of them sleeping in this small room and so few places to store things.

Makay shut the door and grabbed me with the hand that didn't hold the pizza, squealing softly. For a moment she looked like the almost nineteen-year-old she was. "Who's the hunk? He's beautiful!"

"I'm not sure."

"What?"

"He's the cousin of the boy at the grocery store."

"Oh, I see." But her smile was knowing as she took another bite.

"There's nothing going on. I just met him." I took out my phone and checked the time.

"Well, there should be. Look how well he gets along with the girls."

"Yeah, maybe too well." Seeing how much they'd been hurt—mostly by men—I wasn't sure letting him get close to them was a good idea. I didn't even know him.

Makay frowned. "You're probably right. Still, there have to be some great guys left in the world, right?"

"Maybe."

There was a hurt in her face that I knew was because of her father, who'd become an alcoholic after her mother died. Makay's life had gone downhill from then, and by twelve she'd pretty much been on her own, sleeping at friends' houses or in parks. That hadn't stopped her from somehow finishing high school, but she'd flunked out of college last semester because she'd missed too much class taking care of Nate.

"So how's Fern?"

Makay's expression sobered. "Actually, that's what I want to talk to you about. She's getting worse. Ever since my dad died, she's like an accident waiting to happen. I'm scared about what this'll mean to Nate. I mean, it's not like he's a newborn and isn't aware of what's going on. He needs me." She paused and said, her voice almost angry, "He's mine, but you know they'll never let me keep him. So I can't call anyone about Fern. I just have to keep him with me and hope she straightens up."

"You're doing the right thing. Nate needs you."

Tears gathered in her eyes. "I love him so much. I'd give anything for him not to go through what I went through, but Fern, she won't sign him over to me. She doesn't care about anything except her next fix. So I just have to keep taking him back to visit whenever she calls." She sighed and added, "I can do this. I have to." She nodded hard, as if to convince herself.

"You can," I said. "And I'll help. We'll help each other."

"You have already. A lot." She grinned suddenly.

"You'd better get going with your shower. I need to run back to my place and get some clothes for Nate, and something to eat. I doubt there'll be any pizza left by the time he wakes."

I laughed. "I'm sure of that."

When I emerged from the bathroom, I found Jameson waiting for me in the tiny kitchen that adjoined the living room. Surprisingly, he and Ruth were washing dishes. Halla was playing with Nate, who'd awakened, her shaved head bent close to his.

"I got it from here," Ruth said to Jameson. "But thanks for the help." He nodded and pulled his hands from the suds.

"Can you make sure Zoey and Bianca do their homework?" I said to Ruth. I usually drove the sisters to school in the mornings, but they had to find their own way home, or call me when I was off work.

"Sure." Ruth smiled. "Oh, and Saffron called your phone when you was in the shower. She says she's coming home, but she ain't gonna be here in time for you to take the car to work."

"That's okay." I'd already texted my sister. "I have a ride. Call me if you need me." We couldn't afford more cell phones, but there was a pay phone at the Circle K they could use.

Ruth rolled her eyes. "It's Wednesday, right? So you only work four hours. What could happen?"

Right. I swept up my purse and headed for the door.

I tried to ignore Jameson as he said goodbye to the girls and followed me, but every one of my senses was on high alert. What was he thinking? Somehow I had to make sure that he didn't run off and call social services or whatever.

He didn't say anything all the way downstairs, and when he started to speak at the bottom of the steps, I shook my head and urged him to walk with me. I'd asked my sister to pick me up at the Circle K, so I wouldn't have to wait for her to come all the way to the apartment, and I wanted to get there before she did. Plus, I didn't want any of my neighbors hearing whatever he planned to say.

The day was beautiful, not too hot now that I wasn't on the roof, and the sky was filled with fat, puffy clouds that reminded me of teddy bears and fabric softener. Of commercials where mothers made cinnamon rolls for their children to eat after school.

I'd always wanted one of those rolls, or at least the mother who went with them.

When we were partway down the street between another apartment complex and a gas station, I glanced up at Jameson. "Well?"

"Well, what?"

"I know you have questions."

He stopped walking, forcing me to also come to a stop. "Oh, I have a lot of questions. Fortunately, Ruth and Halla answered most of them."

"No they didn't." The girls knew how to keep their mouths shut. Inside our apartment, we told each other everything, but not to outsiders, no matter how charming or good-looking, because that meant danger. I'd found both Ruth and Halla while serving Thanksgiving dinner to the homeless at a church here in Phoenix where we still attended on Sundays, and I was glad I'd overheard them talking about where they'd sleep, or they might have ended up in danger. They had just as much to lose if they were discovered as Elsie, and they were expert at keeping secrets. Whatever they'd talked about with Jameson, it hadn't been anything real.

He blew out a breath of frustration. "You're right. They didn't say anything." His jaw worked, but he fell silent as a Hispanic woman pushing a stroller passed us by. A car brake squealed as a driver slowed enough to pull into the gas station, and the sound was like an alarm reminding me that I needed to hurry, or I'd be late to work—again.

When the woman was gone, Jameson said, "What they didn't say told me a lot more than what they did. Look, they need help. You know that, right?"

Fury waved through me. How dare he judge me from just this little bit that he'd seen. "Okay, stop right there. You know nothing about where they've been and what they've gone through."

"I know more than you think. The system can help them."

"You're wrong! *The system* has already failed!" Stupid tears started as I fumbled in my pocket for my phone. "Ruth was sexually assaulted by two of her mother's boyfriends, and *the system* kept putting her back there— and her mother doesn't even want her, hasn't even reported her missing. And Halla? She was starved into submission by her drunk father. No one believed her, and she was locked in a room for six months until she finally jumped out her window and broke her arm. She escaped from the hospital after her father convinced everyone it was an accident and not attempted suicide."

Jameson's eyes widened, but he didn't look as surprised as I expected. Maybe he didn't believe me.

There was much more. "Two of the girls you didn't meet? I only got guardianship of them to stop their uncle from molesting them. The oldest still cuts herself when she's stressed. And Elsie . . ." Finally, I found the picture on the phone and shoved it into his face. "This is what she looked like when Payden and I found her in back of the store. Ask him if you don't believe me. If you're going to send her back to the monster that did this, I need to know that now." The tears skidded down both cheeks, but I didn't care. These were my girls.

"Because you'd all disappear."

I didn't reply, but he was right. I had a few hundred that would keep us at a cheap motel for a few nights, at least. Tessa and Makay would help me figure out what to do then.

Jameson slowly gave me back the phone. "Anyway, that's not what I meant. I want to help, and there are ways to get that from the system."

"How?" I asked. "*After* I lose the girls? I'm the only family they have. The *only* stability. I know it's not a lot, but it's more than where they came from."

I knew because I'd grown up in a family with money, and I felt more love in my dingy, rundown apartment with runaways than I ever had in my parents' million-dollar house. "I'm twenty-two. I haven't even graduated from college. I have a part-time job that I'm lucky to have because it pays me triple minimum wage, but it isn't enough."

Another tear fell, and I wiped it away impatiently. The tears came only from frustration, because inside I was strong and my resolve was hardening. The girls and I could pack fast. He didn't know my last name or the name of the girls I had guardianship over. He'd never find where we'd gone. No more groceries from Payden, but that couldn't be helped.

A young couple passed us on the street, giving us a sidelong stare. "I'm okay," I told them. "We're just breaking up." They nodded, looking embarrassed, and continued walking.

"Breaking up?" Jameson gawked at me, one side of his beautiful mouth twitching upward. "Oh, no, Lily. We're just beginning."

"What?" My turn to gawk.

"I went to the store today because Payden told me about what you'd done for Elsie. I came because I wanted to see if I could help you and her."

No wonder he'd just *happened* to be there in time to help me carry the box. "If you really want to help, you'll just leave us alone. I told Payden I didn't need you."

I started to walk back in the direction of the apartment to pack up the girls, but he grabbed my hand. "Wait, Lily. Please."

Something in his voice made me stop. Or was it his touch? Because it was warm and made my heart pound, but it also felt strangely . . . familiar.

"I have no intention of reporting you or the girls."

"Really?" I met his eyes, searching for signs of deceit.

"Believe it or not, I do understand. I've seen parents do things they shouldn't, and I've seen kids getting lost in the paperwork." A crease appeared between his eyes, and for a brief instant, his eyes had the same haunted look that I still found far too often in Elsie's. "But I also know you can do a lot more for these girls with the system on your side instead of working against you." He paused for a minute, thinking. He hadn't let go of my hand, and I didn't pull away. "The first thing to do is get you licensed as a foster parent. Then we'll see what you can do from there."

"You can't know how much I want that." I didn't mean it to come out as a whisper. "To be legitimate."

"I think I do. I've been to your crummy apartment."

I slowly took my hand from Jameson's, because we weren't together and ultimately it was my problem, not his. "I'm not sure where to begin. I've still got a couple years left of school, maybe more if I change majors again." I wasn't even sure if the college would give me more than another year of scholarships.

"Foster parenting isn't about school, it's more about learning skills to deal with kids in crisis. I work at a place called Teen Remake, and we offer classes that count with the Department of Child Safety. It's for anyone who'd like to be a foster parent or work with kids, even for those of us who don't want to major in social work. I could get you hooked up if you're interested. Plus, there are other opportunities to learn or be involved. They step up their programs during the summer months and always need more help—and not just for volunteers. There are paid openings. Call me, and we'll figure out a time for you to go in." He reached in his back pocket and from his wallet pulled out a card that listed his name and his accounting services.

"You work in their program or do their accounting?" I asked.

"Actually, both. I started out helping with their budgeting. Then I got interested in the programs. I've been there three years now, two full time, but I'm dropping down to part time again when I go back to school this fall to finish my degree."

"If I go, my girls stay out of it?"

He nodded. "For now."

That irritated me. Who did he think he was? But the offer of a license was temptation enough to overlook a lot. What should I do? There was no one really to ask besides Tessa, and if I was honest, she usually came to me for advice these days.

"Okay," I said finally. "I'd like to try." Being legit was everything.

"It helps that you have guardianship over two of the girls. Their relatives must trust you."

"Actually, their uncle had custody, and I threatened to tell the police that he tried to rape me if he didn't agree to give me guardianship so I could put them in school." I met Jameson's eyes straight on. "He was guilty of more than attempted rape. Just not with me."

Jameson's nostrils flared and his fists clenched. I could just imagine his opinion of me falling a couple more notches on his measuring stick. Well, I'd already determined that it wouldn't work out between us.

"I doubt he's going to cry blackmail if he's already given you the girls. How long have you had them?"

"Five months."

"They doing well in school?"

"Better than before."

Jameson smiled, and my stomach did the same funny dance it had when I'd come down with the stomach flu. *It's the girls he's interested in helping,* I told myself. He'd only come to the store to check on Elsie. The rest had been a smokescreen.

My theory was blown to bits when his hand moved slowly to wipe the tear from under my left eye. The sound of traffic faded and it was just us, as if someone had sucked away all the sound and everything around us to another dimension.

"I don't know what I'd expected when Payden first told me about you, but you're much more than anything I thought up." His voice lowered as he added, "I think you're even a bit amazing."

His words were so unexpected, I couldn't even blink. His eyes drank me in. One part of my mind knew there were cars in the street and people nearby, but I couldn't sense any of them.

Jameson's hand dropped. "With all that stuff out of the way, let's get down to the most important thing—will you go out with me?"

As I ran to meet Tessa's car, a vision of Jameson doing dishes with Ruth kept pushing into my mind. She hadn't been cringing or afraid of him. Even Elsie had taken a slice of his pizza. Didn't that say something?

I didn't want to put a lot of trust in him, but it was too late to worry about that now. Standing on the sidewalk looking into those eyes had made all the romantic dreams I'd tried to squash come roaring to life. I believed him.

Tessa peeked at her phone as I slipped into the passenger seat of her compact Toyota. "You're going to be late."

"I know. I'm sorry."

"Don't tell me. It's the people on your lines who might start asking questions."

I shrugged. "They'll think I'm in a meeting. Besides, I've got them all well-trained. Everything should run smoothly for a few minutes without me." I tried not to think about the dull hours ahead, watching my line workers as they hurried to meet their daily quota. I suspected that moving me from accounting to line supervisor was a punishment for transferring out of the business classes my father had been adamant I should take. The lines were boring and tedious, but in the end, I was good at it because it was only a matter of organization. Managing workers was far easier than taking care of my girls.

Tessa didn't reply as she concentrated on pulling into traffic. She was two years older, and growing up we'd been inseparable. College, work, and different interests had changed that a little, but not enough to make a difference. She'd always been a constant in my life. She liked to joke that someone had upended a bucket of orange paint on her head, but I thought her "strawberry blond" hair was stunning. I also loved the freckles that blotted most of her face. I'd tried counting them as a child but had given up after ninety-nine. I'd always been annoyed that I had blond hair and only seven freckles.

"What?" she said, apparently feeling my stare.

"Thanks for coming."

"What happened to your car anyway?"

"I lent it to Saffron. She had a job interview."

Tessa laughed. "Are you sure she's going to bring it back?"

There was that. "Unless something spooks her, she will. She's only got two more months before she's eighteen. She's actually very reliable."

Tessa frowned as she glanced in the rearview mirror. "How's she doing?"

"A lot better. She's been going to those free counseling sessions at that church near the college."

Saffron's family had kicked her out when she'd turned

up expecting last year. She'd survived several months on the street before she lost the baby—and her hope. She'd crashed after that, blaming the baby's death on herself. One day she took too many sleeping pills to end the pain. Fortunately, I found her passed out in a classroom at the college where she'd been sleeping during the days, trying to blend in with the regular students. After I took her to the hospital for emergency care, where she refused to tell them her real name, she'd had nowhere to go and ended up staying with me in my old apartment.

"So glad for her. She's lucky she has you. All of the girls are." Tessa glanced at me and then back to the road, her mouth curving in a smile.

I wanted to tell Tessa about the move and about Jameson, but something pressed deeper on my mind. "I just need a bigger place."

"You mean something like that house you used to dream about."

"Oh, I still dream about it." I laid my head back on the seat and sighed. "A big house with a ton of rooms and a big yard. It can be old and rundown, and full of weeds. Or have broken siding or old wallpaper."

"Even a green fridge?"

I laughed. "Even a green fridge, because none of that matters. It's full of love and music and fun."

Tessa laughed with me. "Are the girls there in this dream?"

"Of course! It's all for them."

Tessa bit her lip, and this time when she glanced over, I saw the tears glistening there. "I remember us talking about it at night when we were kids. You'd come and snuggle in my bed with me."

When Mom and Dad were screaming, she meant. Fighting over my father's lies. I reached out and touched her leg. "I'm going to do it! As soon as I get Grandpa's money, I'll find a place. Or before if I can find something I can afford." A house without lies—that was my dream.

"I'll help," Tessa said.

I clapped my hands, startling her with the noise. "Right! You could get the money next year. Well, if you hurry and get married."

"There is that." She grimaced. "But that's probably not going to happen. We'd better stick with plan A."

"Either way, I'm going to make it happen."

Tessa nodded and grinned. "I know you will."

"Speaking of houses, I've been meaning to tell you that I moved."

"What!" She did a double take at me before looking back at the street.

"Yeah, some of my old roommates got upset when I brought Elsie home. I couldn't exactly hide her, since she was all beaten up and I had to carry her inside. But at this place, we don't have to sneak around all the time."

"Why didn't you tell me? I would have helped you move."

"We didn't have much—just a couple of car loads—and it happened so fast. We're at the same place as Makay now. It's a dump, but we have a lot more room." I laughed as I said it. Who would have ever thought I'd call that tiny apartment more room?

We pulled up at Crawford Cereals, and Tessa leaned over to hug me. "Have I ever told you how proud I am of you? You're like a light in this dark world—that's why those girls trust you so much and want to do anything you say."

I laughed suddenly, feeling more positive than I had in weeks. "Well, they don't do everything I say, but I'm working on it. Anyway, I'm proud of you, too. You're the one who changed my diapers when you were only a baby yourself, and made sure I was safe. I'm probably alive because of you."

I didn't add that she'd been all I'd had growing up, but we both knew it. Or at least after our grandfather had died. Our mother had been into charities and entertaining, not children. And our father, well, he was into work and money. There had been a series of housekeepers after the nanny left when I was two, but they weren't the loving, motherly kind you read about in story books. Mother liked to hire efficient and silent help.

"Grandfather never would have made you wait for the money if he were still alive," Tessa said. "You know he did that because of how Dad was when he was young. He wanted to make sure the money wouldn't ruin us."

"Maybe he's right. It'll mean more once we get it." I hugged her. "But I'll have the house before then. You'll see." I started to get out of the car, then paused. "I almost forgot to tell you. I met someone."

"No way." Tessa's eyes grew large. I could see the darker blue ring around her iris and the gold flecks near the pupils, like shimmering freckles. It was like looking into my own eyes and practically the only thing that marked us as sisters.

"What do you mean, no way?"

"It was how your face looked when you said 'I met someone.' Like it was important. What's his name?"

"Most people call him Mario, but I call him Jameson. He asked me out and I said maybe. I'll have to explain it all some other time, or I'll be even more late." I slammed the door.

"You'd better!" she called, her voice muffled now. I waved and ran to the factory.

Inside, my lines and all my workers were in chaos. One of the packing machines had broken down, and the cereal boxes had been misprinted. But in ten minutes, I had new boxes delivered, and all but the broken line functioning. Fifteen minutes after that, the machine was fixed.

To make up for the lost time, I planned to fill in at each station as the workers took their breaks. We'd still make our minimum quota that way, but my father had already peeked in the room, and he didn't look happy. I knew I should have been there on time, but I didn't know how to change that. The girls had to come first. Unfortunately, working the line myself meant I'd have to do my quarterly employee reviews and my other reports at home.

Fleetingly, my thoughts went to Jameson and getting licensed as a foster parent. Maybe that would work out. He'd also said the company might be hiring, and I'd give almost anything to work anywhere but here, even though the factory was my beloved grandfather's legacy. But

Grandfather had left his own father's law firm to start this factory, so he'd understand.

My phone buzzed as I was walking to relieve the third employee, and I picked up, feeling trepidation when I didn't recognize the number. "Hello?"

"Lily! Good, you answered."

"Ruth? Is everything okay?" The last time they'd called me at work was when Zoey had been sent home early from school for fighting. There was always the chance that Jameson had reported us, though the girls knew well enough not to open the door to strangers, so there might be time to salvage things if that was the case. The thought made my mouth go dry.

"I just had to tell you!" Ruth gave a little squeal. "Some delivery guy came with flowers. At first we wasn't gonna open the door, but Saffron was home and she had us hide while she answered. And they turned out to be flowers for you! White lilies. A whole dozen of them! And we opened the card—sorry, we couldn't wait."

"Who are they from?"

"Someone named Jameson?"

Relief cut through my anxiety. "Oh, good."

"Who's Jameson? We thought they might be from Mario, since it's obvious he's totally in love with you. You holding out on us, girl?"

I laughed. "No, Mario is Jameson. I just call him that."

"Ooooh, I get it. A secret nickname."

"Not secret. His mother uses it."

"Always best to make nice with the mother, I say."

"I haven't even met his mother."

"Oh, you will. I have no doubt. Well, I gotta go. I'm going to vacuum the apartment. See you later."

Vacuum? Ruth was the mothering kind, but she didn't ordinarily do Saffron's job. In fact, most of the girls still had trouble getting their chores finished without my nagging. I'd have to look into that later. Ruth seemed happier than I thought she'd be about my dating someone. She usually showed nothing but revulsion for any male we encountered, including Saffron's frequent dates.

Jameson had sent me flowers.

I waited until my own break to call the number on the card he'd pushed into my hand, and he picked up on the second ring. "Okay," I told him. "I'll go out with you. No nicknames though. I'm confused enough about what to call you."

"Great!" he said. "Unfortunately, I met this girl today, and I'm crazy about her. She has the most amazing eyes, and she knows how to climb roofs. In fact, I've been waiting for her call, but she didn't give me her number, so I won't even know it's her if she calls. Do you think I'm waiting for nothing?"

A laugh bubbled up inside me. "I don't think so. Maybe I could give her a message for you?"

"Really? Will you ask her if I can pick her up tonight at six? Will that be too soon do you think?"

A thrill shot through me; he wasn't wasting any time. "It's cutting it short, but I think she'll be home."

"Okay. Tell her I'll see her then. Tell her it's for dinner."

"I'm sure she'll love that." My stomach growled at the thought. During the chaos today, I hadn't even snagged a piece of pizza. I'd have to run by Tessa's office to see if she had any food stashed in her desk.

Jameson hadn't hung up, so I hurried to say, "Thanks for the flowers."

He laughed. "Ah, the magic of flowers. Never fails."

"Right. Especially lilies. Remember that."

"Oh, I will."

"See you tonight."

When I arrived at the apartment, the living room looked surprisingly organized for a change. The blankets that were usually in mounds had been folded into a huge stack on the couch, and two more Walmart fold-out mattresses, like the ones in the bedroom, had been doubled into soft, distorted chairs. Ruth and Halla slept on those, while I used the couch, but often the other girls would crash with us instead of in the bedroom, if they fell asleep in front of the small television. That meant it normally looked like a bomb had gone off unless I was home to make everyone clean up.

"I got the job!" Saffron grabbed me and twirled me around.

"That's great! When do you start?"

"Monday." She grinned and pulled her hand through her hair, the color a pale version of Tessa's, which was how Saffron had chosen her nickname. No one called her Rosalyn, her real name, or she threatened to kill them.

"I'm a little worried about clothing. I mean, I know it's

only a mall kiosk, but I need to look cool to sell things."
She looked at me pleadingly.

I laughed. "Yes, you can borrow my clothes." That was
one thing I didn't lack because every time I went home,
my mother took me out shopping for whatever event she
was throwing. Instead of protesting, I'd taken to buying
things that were bigger or smaller than my real size, and
then passing them on to the girls. Saffron was a good ten
pounds thinner than I was—but it was close enough.

"Can you help me with my hair that morning?"

"Sure. I'll even drop you off the first day, but you'll
have to buy the bus pass for the rest of the time."

"I stopped and bought a pass on the way home." She
laughed. "I can't believe I'm going to be selling jewelry
and scarves. Me! No more slinging hamburgers."

I didn't remind her that her hamburger job had helped
us with the down payment on this apartment, but I did
remember how easily she'd offered, even though I knew
she was saving up for a car.

The white lilies on the kitchen counter caught my
attention, and I leaned over to smell them. Anticipation
tingled through me at the thought of seeing Jameson
tonight. "Where are the girls?" I had a little over an hour
before he was supposed to be here, and I needed to make
sure they had dinner.

"They took Nate to the park. Makay's going to meet
them there to pick him up. Don't worry. Zoey and Bianca
did their homework before Ruth let them go." Saffron
made a face. "Elsie stayed home, though. She's in the
bedroom. She's acting funny."

"She had a scare this morning. I'd better go talk to her." I hurried down the hall and opened the door slowly.

Inside, I found the same organization that prevailed in the living room. The blankets were tucked nicely around the double mattress and also around the two fold-out beds. Today the path around the beds was perfectly clean.

Elsie was curled on top of her blue fold-out mattress, the one I'd used before her arrival, her tangled hair fanned around her. A faded pink backpack that held most of her belongings sat near her flattened pillow, and she cuddled a small stuffed wolf I'd bought for her the day after I found her.

I felt a momentary dismay that she had so little. How different from the way I'd grown up, surrounded by dolls, toys, stuffed animals, and electronic gadgets. I'd had thirty-one nail polishes that I rarely used, and even lip glosses to put into every one of the dozen purses my mother had bought for me.

That's not love, I reminded myself. Love had been Tessa reading to me every day for the two months I'd been sick during the year I was supposed to have started kindergarten.

I went around to Elsie's mattress and sat next to her. She opened her eyes, but she didn't return my smile. "Is everything okay?" I asked.

She nodded and scooted closer, which I took as an invitation to put my arm around her. She gave a soft sigh and let her head rest on my lap. Absently, I started smoothing her hair but stopped before she pulled away. Elsie's hair desperately needed attention, but she refused to let anyone style it. While I believed she washed her head once a week, she never combed her hair or used conditioner, and her dark mane was nearly as frizzy as Ruth's when it wasn't in braids. The frizz didn't look bad on Ruth, but on Elsie, it was all wrong.

I stroked her cheek, so pale under the still-fading green bruises. I needed to get her out of the house and soon, before her reluctance became a phobia.

"Is he coming here again?" she asked in a small voice. "Mario, I mean."

I tried to think of the best way to respond. I needed to know what was bothering her so much that she was curled here in a ball instead of out in the living room reading the books I'd borrowed at the library or watching her allotted television time. "Would that bother you?"

She hesitated, giving a little sigh. "I don't know. He was nice. But I'm afraid *he's* going to find me."

"He?" Obviously, she didn't mean Jameson. "Do you want to talk about him? About what happened before I found you?"

She shook her head. "Do you like Mario?"

"Well. He seems nice, and he promised he wouldn't say anything about us. Is that what's bothering you?"

One shoulder lifted in a shrug.

"It's okay to feel that way after what you've been through, and I don't know him myself that well yet, so I can't say he's a good person, but Payden says he is."

"I like Payden."

"So do I. You know, he asked after you today. I told him you might come with me on Friday." We went every other day to pick up expired groceries, and telling her now gave her the rest of today and tomorrow to think about it.

"Maybe."

"One important thing is that Jameson—or Mario, as everyone calls him—works with some therapists. They can help me become licensed so I can keep girls like you for real."

"You mean you'd be their guardian? Like you are for Zoey and Bianca?"

"Even better. Guardianship basically just lets me put them in school and take care of them, but I don't get money from the state or from their uncle. I've just been too happy for that much to push for anything else. I worry if the state tried to take them permanently from their uncle, he'd fight for them. Or the state might not place them with me, especially living in this little apartment. It'd be awful for Zoey and Bianca to have to start over again."

"It's not bad here. I love it."

Once more, a deep sense of sadness filled me that having so little meant so much to her. While I wanted Elsie to feel safe, this wasn't the dream I had for her and the others. No, I wanted more.

"But if I meet someone where Mario works, someone we could trust, who can see that you're safe with me and could maybe help us, it would be a good thing, right?"

"What if they want to send me back?"

She had the right to ask. "Well, I'm not saying I'd tell them about you right away. I'd want to feel them out, see what the policies are and everything. Then if I felt it was safe, I'd figure out things for Zoey and Bianca first, since they're already with me officially. Then we'd go from there and figure out the rest."

"What if it doesn't work?"

"I have emergency money in the bank, and I'll take you somewhere safe."

She knew this routine. We talked about it enough. "The park?"

"The park bench by the big tree is just where we'll meet, if we get separated. Then we'll go to a hotel, or stay with Tessa or Makay. But I'll be careful, I promise."

Elsie didn't reply, but she appeared to be considering my words.

I snuggled closer. "You know, my sister reminded me of something today. When I was even younger than you, we used to sit together in bed at night and talk about our dreams. And you know what my dream was?"

Elsie twisted her neck to look up at me, her brown eyes eager. "What?"

"A big house with a big yard. A house with tons of kids and more love than you could ever need. You could snuggle on the couch with your feet on it without anyone getting upset, and there would be a wall where we could put handprints or draw pictures, and someone would also be cooking something that tasted good, and we didn't always have to eat all our vegetables before we had dessert. And when people got upset, everyone would hug them until they were happy again. No one would tell lies, but we'd make up plenty of fun stories to share. There would be lots of music and laughter. Oh, we'd still have to brush our teeth and do chores—we don't want to live in a pigsty—but no one would yell about it. And if mud came in on our shoes, we'd just laugh and clean it up. We could sleep outside on the grass if we wanted and have a pit where we could roast marshmallows. We'd probably have pets too, just for fun. Maybe rabbits to make fertilizer in case we want a garden."

Elsie's mouth opened in a laugh that didn't quite escape her throat. "And no one would use belts for hitting, and I could eat as much cheese as I want. I like that."

My gut clenched at the belt comment, but I knew better than to pursue it. "So that's what's happening to all our cheese?" I started tickling her.

She laughed aloud then, and hearing her made me happy.

"But, Lily," she said, her expression sobering, "we already have that all right here, don't we? No one yells, and we get enough food, and even when the girls argue about jobs, they never hit."

I had to clamp my mouth hard for a moment not to burst into tears at how she saw things. "Well, I guess you're right, except I want a few more rooms, and we can't fit a horse in here yet."

She giggled. "A dog?"

"The landlord won't let us, but I bet I could find big sheets of paper to put on the wall for us to draw on."

We lay there quietly, thinking about that for a while. Then Elsie said, "So Mario might be able to help?"

"I think so."

"You should try then."

I knew what it cost her to say it. I hugged her tighter.

"Halla and Ruth said he was hot," she added. "Do *you* think he's hot?"

"Whew! I'll say." I pretended to fan my face. "I'm thinking I might have to start carrying ice cubes in my pockets."

Elsie grinned again, making me feel like I'd won the lottery. "Everyone can tell he likes you, so maybe he's the one who needs the ice."

I laughed. "Maybe so." We heard a door shut, followed by voices. "Looks like the others are home, and I have to get dinner ready. I've got a date tonight."

"With hot guy?"

"Yep, but let's go start the tuna salad." Makay had found tuna coupons that made the cans nearly free a few months ago, and we'd stocked up. Great source of protein, but I had to admit I was a little sick of tuna.

I started the water boiling in the kitchen, put Ruth in charge of the noodles, and set Halla opening cans. Then I went to the bathroom and let Elsie comb my hair. I added a little lip gloss.

"Do you think I should wear my pink blouse?" I asked her.

"Yeah. You look really pretty in that."

After changing, I returned to the living room. Saffron tore her gaze away from the blaring television long enough to say, "You going somewhere? Because if you're going out on a date, you need more makeup."

Next to her on the couch, sixteen-year-old Zoey looked up, shifting her bulk awkwardly. Her weight and the heavy makeup were a mask every bit as much Ruth's layers of clothing.

"Nope, she's taking us to the art display tonight at

school." She said something in rapid Spanish to her too-thin sister, Bianca, who was a year younger but attended the same high school.

Bianca nodded emphatically. "Yep, it's tonight. We get extra credit for going."

That's right. I'd completely forgotten. They each had a piece of pottery on display, and they needed any help they could get with their grades.

That was when the doorbell rang. No doubt it was "hot guy," and I was going to have to send him away.

I pushed aside disappointment as Halla sprinted to look out the peephole. Go with the flow, was my motto. I just hoped Jameson was still willing to help me when I put him off again. It's not as if I was really interested in starting a relationship. Okay, maybe I was, but I shouldn't be, not with my responsibilities.

"It's him!" Halla said in a loud whisper. "He's back. Mario or Jameson, or whatever we're going to call him."

"He's Lily's date," Elsie said, her voice sounding loud in the sudden quiet.

Everyone stared at me. "You're going out with him?" Saffron gave a smile of approval. "Cool."

"No, not anymore."

Halla looked over from the door. "Should I open it?"

"Is anyone with him?" Ruth asked.

Good girl, I thought. "Let me get it, okay? Is the food ready?"

Ruth nodded. "We have stuff for s'mores, too, for watching Nate today. Makay gets a kick out of how we roast marshmallows over the electric burners." The girls murmured approval, but no one started for the stove.

"Well?" Halla said. "Aren't you going to answer it?" They waited expectantly, their faces bright, except Elsie, who rolled her eyes and ran toward the bedroom.

Halla moved aside, and I pushed her toward the kitchen area before opening the door. I caught my breath just a little as I saw him. Dark jeans, a black and gray short-sleeved shirt with buttons and a collar, his hair combed back, his face newly shaven. His eyes seemed to pull me in, and for a long instant, I couldn't speak.

"You going to invite me in?" he asked.

I shook my head. "We ran into a little problem."

"Well, we can talk about it while we put these away." He handed me a heavy plastic sack and bent over for a box I hadn't noticed. Plump yellow grapefruit filled the entire thing, and I peeked in the sack to reveal more of the same.

"My mother was in town," Jameson explained. "She doesn't think I get enough fruit, and apparently my neighbor's grapefruit trees were ready to harvest. I kept some, but I can't eat more than one a day. Girls like this stuff, right?"

He looked so anxious, I had to laugh. "Come on in."

The girls were all eating tuna salad, sitting or standing around the small table. "Anyone like grapefruit?" I asked.

"Me," chimed Saffron and Ruth, while Zoey and Bianca nodded. Only Halla wrinkled her small nose.

"I knew they'd save me," Jameson said.

"From death by grapefruit." Zoey snagged one of the fruits from Jameson's box.

He grinned. "Something like that."

"I need to lose a little weight anyway," she said. "I think there's such a thing as a grapefruit diet."

"Knock yourself out." He set the box on the counter.

"Thanks," I told Jameson. "I'll put as many as I can in the fridge later."

"Hey, Lily, I want to go to the art show. Can I?" Ruth stood by the stove with a bowl of tuna salad close to her face, her fork shoveling it in. Someday I'd get around to teaching her etiquette, but for now, her grammar was going to be my next focus.

Halla nodded. "Me too."

"Not me." Saffron made a face. "No offense, but I'll wait to see their stuff when you bring it home. High schools make me claustrophobic."

Zoey smirked. "You think *I'd* go if I didn't have to?" Saffron laughed, and the girls bumped fists.

"Art show?" Jameson looked at me. "Is that what you were going to tell me?"

I rummaged in the cupboard, searching for another bowl to put tuna salad in. "Yes. Zoey and Bianca have pottery in the art show tonight at the high school."

"It's so lame," Zoey added. "But we get extra credit if we go."

"I think my piece is kind of cool," Bianca said in way that told me it meant a lot more to her than she was letting on.

Jameson checked his watch. "I bet it is. What time does it start? Seven?" When she nodded, he said, "Mind if I tag along?"

I stared. "You want to go?"

"I love art."

Bianca's grin spread across her thin face. "Sure, you can come. Do you know how to throw pots?"

"Not exactly, but I'd like to learn." He held up a finger. "Wait a minute, I've got to run down to my car and bring something up."

Ruth was already sticking a marshmallow on the end of a metal hanger. "So, this means it's still a date, right?" she said when Jameson was gone.

"With all of you along?" Saffron gave a snort. "I'd like to see him try to give her a goodnight kiss."

She had a point.

Zoey rolled her eyes. "We'll look the other way. Give me some of those." She grabbed for the bag of marshmallows.

"What happened to your grapefruit diet?" Ruth held them out of her reach.

"Shut your stupid trap! And give 'em to me!"

"Fine, but this time I ain't cleaning up if you drop your marshmallows off the hanger." Ruth relinquished the bag, but Halla grabbed it from Zoey's hands.

The girls were still involved in a friendly game of keep-away with the bag of marshmallows when Jameson returned carrying a picnic basket that looked like something from a classical movie.

"I have chicken salad," he called, setting the basket on the counter and pulling out a large plastic container. "And croissants."

"More salad?" Ruth moaned.

Saffron let her fork clatter to the table as she abandoned her dinner. "Hey, at least it's not tuna."

"Did you make these?" I examined the container of croissants, which smelled delicious. Obviously, this had been part of our planned date tonight, and with regret, I wondered where he might have taken me so we could enjoy it together. I had a sneaking suspicion the girls had disclosed how much I utterly adored croissants.

"I could tell you yes," he said, "but then I'd be lying. I bought it all at a deli near my house."

"Lily doesn't let us lie," Ruth said.

Saffron rolled her eyes. "He's kidding." She grabbed the bowl of chicken salad. "I'll try some."

"Lily first." Jameson passed the salad to me, and I was only happy to spread some on one of the rolls.

"Wow," I said, forgetting that my mouth was full. "It's really good."

"The secret is in the spices, or so they say." He layered a healthy spoonful of the mixture on another roll for himself before passing it to the girls. "Save Elsie one," he warned.

He'd remembered her! I stepped back and glanced down the hall, just in time to see the door to the bedroom click shut. Evidently, Elsie wasn't as indifferent to his visit as she pretended.

When I looked back at Jameson, he was helping the girls with their sandwiches. I offered him an apologetic grin. "Sorry about all the chaos. But it never really gets any quieter here."

"It's exactly like home. Remember, I have five siblings." Behind him, Saffron was pulling a bottle from the basket, but Jameson's hand shot out to stop her. "Sorry, that's not for kids."

"Oh, beans," she said. "Lily never has alcohol here. Can't even sneak it like I used to at my parents' house."

"Exactly," I said. "If I don't have it, you guys can't sneak it." Ruth in particular had a weakness for alcohol, a genetic predisposition I was sure she'd gotten from her mother, and I had to keep a close eye on her.

"Good thing I have chocolate mousse, which is even better." Jameson pulled out a small bowl, and everyone dived for a spoon.

Jameson chuckled. "It's like feeding time at the zoo. Next time, I'll bring more."

Next time. The words sent anticipation tingling through my body. "Right." I reached over for my purse. "Come on, everyone. Time to hit the road."

Jameson took us in his car, which turned out to be a red Mustang that was far older than the new Honda my parents had bought for me years earlier, but his paint was new, and with the bench seat in front, it fit all six of us. The bench seat was very rare, we were told, and Jameson had restored the car with his dad as a teen. Zoey gave him directions to the school from the front seat, while I sat between them trying not to be so aware of Jameson's thigh against mine. It didn't help that he kept glancing over at me every few seconds.

"Do I have chicken salad in my teeth?" I finally asked at a light, stretching to see the mirror.

His smile made my stomach flop. "No. But you do have a little mousse here." He touched the corner of my mouth, wiped slowly, and then licked his finger. "Mmm, even better."

He might as well have kissed me for the response in my body. I wanted to lean forward and let him kiss me for real.

"That is totally gross," Ruth said, ruining the moment. Halla and Bianca howled with laughter.

"I'm glad you think so," Jameson said. "Because I don't want to share." That made me turn red, and the girls laugh harder. His hand slipped over mine where it lay on my thigh, and except for shifting gears, it didn't leave until we arrived at the high school.

Inside, the school lobby had been transformed with portable walls and tables, where paintings, photographs, sculptures, and pottery were on display. Some of the draw-ings and photographs were quite good, but the pottery was mostly lopsided, malformed, or painted oddly. Four or five looked exactly like pieces I'd done in the third grade, ones my mother had thrown into the trash when she thought I wasn't looking.

Zoey grimaced as she showed her mug that sported an elephant snout and ears. No matter how we tried to stand the mug straight, it kept tipping over. "Yeah, it's pretty bad," she said. "But, hey, it's art credit, and I don't have to play an instrument. The class is pretty fun."

"Where's yours?" I asked Bianca.

Her eyes strayed to a grouping on a table at the end. I immediately saw the difference between these three pieces and the other ones on display. The three made even the best of the other pieces look careless and awkward. One was a short vase, graceful and perfectly formed and painted a vibrant blue. The second was a mug with an elaborately twisted handle, and inside it, a little fairy peering over the side. The final piece was a smooth, nearly flat plate with a swirling design that even my mother probably wouldn't mind hanging on a wall.

"They're beautiful," I said. "Which one's yours?"

Bianca blushed. "They're all mine."

"Incredible!" I hugged her. Bianca loved to draw and always carried a notebook around, but this was a pleasant surprise. "I'm so proud of you!" I reached out and ran a finger along the edge of the plate. "It must have taken forever to get this so straight."

"It did take forever," Zoey said. "Every time I stay after for drama, she's in the art room."

Jameson ripped a couple of twenties from his wallet. "Are they for sale? I want to be the first one to buy one of your originals."

Bianca looked startled. "Uh, no, um . . ." She petered off, her face brilliantly red, a mixture of pleasure and reluctance.

"Of course they aren't for sale!" I slapped his hand away. "But we'll let you know if she changes her mind. Now put that away."

"Hey, guys, I'm getting cookies before they're gone." Ruth made a beeline for the refreshment table, and the other girls dashed after her.

Jameson picked up Bianca's mug. "She really has a talent. If she's got the dedication, she'll be able to make a living with it someday."

"As long as her uncle doesn't hear about it." I paused, and then rushed on, "If she had more opportunities, she could go even further, but I don't have money for extra classes or training . . . or whatever she needs."

He shook his head and carefully set down the piece. "You can't focus on what she doesn't have. There will be opportunities—you just have to keep an eye out for them."

Jameson had a point. I could make sure they let her take more pottery and art classes, and talk to the teacher to see if he was willing to keep letting her come in after school. He must have noticed her talent.

"You're right," I said. "One step at a time." I glanced around the room, but her teacher didn't seem to be here, so I'd have to discuss things with him another night.

"We have other resources and connections at Teen Remake—and we often hook parents up with the additional resources offered by DCS. That's why getting licensed is important." He glanced down at the pieces. "But honestly, if she loves it, she won't give up. As long as anyone doesn't try to force her to become something she hates, she'll be fine."

I thought fleetingly of my parents enrolling me into business classes and how I'd hated them. "You sound like you speak from experience."

He laughed. "Not me. My dad. He worked as an accountant when I was young, but now he does woodworking. Makes almost nothing, but he's happy."

"What about you? Your card says you do accounting."

"That's right. I actually worked with my dad in his shop for a year after high school, but it turned out that while I enjoy working with my hands, I like numbers more. So now I have a year left in college before I dive into an MBA. But I still don't plan to work for anyone but myself in the long run."

"Believe it or not, business was my original plan," I said with a laugh. "But after basic accounting, I was ready to call it quits. Then I studied psychology. And I just finished a year of nursing classes."

"I bet that's all come in very handy with the girls."

"Oh, yeah, but I'm going to change again. I just don't know to what."

"You don't?" He glanced at the girls, who were standing together laughing near the refreshment table. "That surprises me. You seem to have a pretty good idea of what you want for your future."

For a fleeting instant, I thought of telling him about my dream house and helping more girls, but I wasn't ready yet to scare him away. "Some things I do know. It gets complicated when you involve family, at least with mine."

"Oh?" His look invited me to confide more, but I didn't want to waste the night talking about my father's dream of Tessa and me running the factory—or better yet, married to rich husbands who would take over and make him even more money.

"We should grab some cookies before my crew eats them all." As we walked toward the girls, I couldn't help noticing how different they looked from one another. Ruth in her big clothes and baseball cap that didn't quite hide her beauty, towering over the others, her dark skin contrasting sharply with short little Halla's pale skin and shaved blond head. Plump Zoey made almost as drastic a contrast next to thin Bianca. I'd always thought everyone could tell just by looking at them that there was something broken inside—I could see it—but here at the school, in their tight little safety knot, they resembled any of the other kids here.

I took a couple cookies from the table and wrapped them in a napkin. "I already got Elsie and Saffron some," Ruth said with a grin. "Go ahead and eat 'em. They're actually good."

I bit into one. "Ugh, seriously? Good? I guess if you like chocolate-flavored cardboard."

Zoey grabbed a couple more. "They have sugar; what more do you want? Not everyone can make them as good as you."

Jameson made a face, but he finished his cookie. "They are pretty bad."

"Lily makes great cookies," Halla said, rubbing a hand on her camouflage pants. "Seriously."

"Can't wait to taste them." Jameson looked appropriately eager.

On the way home, the girls sang a camp song I'd taught them. I'd gone to two or three camps every summer since I was eight, and I knew all the songs. They scattered from the car when we pulled up in the parking lot at the apartment, Zoey giving catcalls as she left until Ruth hushed her. They hurried up the stairs, past a figure leaning on the second-floor railing, a glowing cigarette in his mouth, his face nearly obscured in the darkness. Only experience told me it was the neighbor who made us all feel uncomfortable, especially Elsie.

"What is it?" Jameson asked, watching them through the windshield.

"Just my neighbor. He was asking Elsie questions the other day. Kind of freaked her out. Then yesterday he followed her to the corner. That's why she was worried when you came today."

"What happened to her?"

I sighed and leaned back on the seat. "She won't talk about it yet. I believe from what little she has said that it was her father who hurt her. She'll talk when she's ready. She has to feel safe first."

"I'm sure you're right."

"I am. They always take time."

After a few moments of silence, he said, "You want to come down to Teen Remake in the morning?"

"Yeah, I have time. I have to drop some of the girls across town at nine, but I can come right after."

"I already talked to our liaison with DCS, who provides oversight for our program, and let her know you're coming in. She'll be there tomorrow, so I can make sure that time works and let you know."

"I'm not telling her about the girls."

He rubbed his hands along the steering wheel. He had nice hands, strong-looking with long fingers, and I could see them working with wood like his father. "I really think you should talk to her at least about Zoey and Bianca. They take sexual assault seriously where teen girls are concerned. I can't see her sending them back to their uncle."

"What if they're sent someplace worse?"

His hands slid down the sides of the steering wheel and rested on his leg. "Naw. They're happy with you, and doing well. There are too many children in the system to worry about something that's working. Trust me on this."

I wanted to trust him because it was what I craved—to give all the girls more. "I'll talk to her."

"You won't regret it."

All at once, I became aware of how close I was still sitting to him. Our eyes met and held. We were parked near the only working streetlight, and the shadows it threw on his face made him appear mysterious and more than a little sensual.

"Sorry about the messed up date," I murmured.

"Don't be." His eyes dipped to my lips.

"I'd better go."

He nodded. "I'll walk you to the door."

"That's okay. I can find my way."

"You should know by now that I'm still going up there—especially with that guy hanging around."

I was tempted to point out that my neighbor was no longer standing by the railing, but I was far more interested in the way he was staring at me. He swallowed hard.

"Okay, you can walk with me," I said.

"All right."

I didn't move and neither did he. Except closer. And closer. I was dying for it to happen. Maybe I had been all day.

He didn't look away. He held my gaze for several heartbeats, giving me every opportunity to pull away. His lips met mine tentatively, as if asking permission, and it was me who moved forward to deepen the kiss. Fire raced through my veins and shuddered through my stomach. A thousand fireworks could have been going off overhead, and I wouldn't have noticed. All the girls could bang on the windows, and I'd keep kissing him.

When we broke apart, he was grinning. I was tempted to pull him back and try again, to wipe off the grin, to daze him as I felt dazed. I'd been kissed before, but this was something incredible.

"Hey, I have an idea," he said. "We can still make our date."

Reality crashed over me. "Tonight? I don't think so. If I don't get the girls in bed, they'll watch television all night, and it's a school night for at least some of them." He might as well learn the truth about my life. There wouldn't be any late night bar-hopping or impromptu road trips. No private movie nights or sleepovers.

"No, I know you have to go in. But how about in the morning? I'll pick you up at five."

"Five?" Was he some kind of maniac? "Who in their right mind ever gets up at five?"

He laughed. "You'll be home in time to get the girls to school. I promise." He looked ready to kiss me again, but I reached for the door. I needed to leave now, or I might regret this later.

"Okay, it's a date." Guess I was just as crazy.

He laughed and jumped out of the Mustang, running around to help me before I had the door halfway open. We raced up four flights, our arms brushing. I tripped him near the door and squeezed into the lead.

"Cheater!"

"Playing to win," I countered.

I stood in front of the door, my heart pounding, keys

to the apartment in my hand. He stepped closer. He was going to kiss me again, and I was going to let him.

Steps pounding up the stairs jolted my attention from Jameson. For a brief instant, fear shuddered through me—and then Ruth and Halla appeared. "Two little lovers sittin' in a tree," they sang.

"Seriously? Are you guys like two?"

They collapsed in laughter against each other. "You didn't even see us," Halla said. "We were spying on you."

I met Jameson's eyes and was grateful to see that he was laughing and not annoyed. "You guys remind me of my little sisters."

"Not Lily," shot Ruth. "You don't kiss sisters like that." Still giggling, they pushed past us, their keys rattling. Light sliced onto Jameson's face from inside the apartment.

"Tomorrow at five," he said, backing away.

"Okay, see you then."

I went inside and found Halla and Ruth recounting everything to the other girls. "Well," Saffron asked, "how was the kiss? A dud? Or fireworks?"

"Definitely fireworks."

Saffron faked seriousness. "Well, then, young lady. I'll have none of *that* in this house. Just so you know."

"It was just a kiss."

"That excuse never works for me," Saffron said with a grin. "Anyway, it must have been some kiss. You took long enough."

I was going to argue, but it had been something amazing, so I took the easy way out and changed the subject. "Well, it's time for bed, everyone." I clapped my hands. "If you get ready fast, we'll watch something."

"Another science show?" Zoey groaned. But she was the first one to the bathroom.

While the girls took turns in the bathroom, I started downloading a science program from the internet for us to watch on the television. I was determined that even those who didn't go to school would learn something. Saffron had taken the GED successfully with my help, even though she'd had to forge her parents' signature to take it, and that was the route we'd go with the others, if we had to.

Sure that everything was in order, I went to check on Elsie. She was reading in the bedroom, curled on her bed. She sat up immediately, her face softly lit by the dim light.

"So, was he mad?" she asked. "About canceling your date, I mean."

"No. And if he was, then it would have been his problem. People don't have the right to be angry about things like that, or at least not to take it out on others."

"Then he'll still help us?"

I put my arm around her. "Yes. I'm going to see a woman at his work tomorrow."

"Is he going to be there?"

"Yes."

Elsie grinned. "Better take some ice."

My hair was still damp when I crept out of the house without awakening the girls. Jameson was just pulling up in the dark parking lot. "So where are we going?" I asked as he jumped out to walk around the car and open my door.

"Well, my plan had been to take you for a sunset picnic. Now it'll be a sunrise."

As if to approve of his plan, my stomach rumbled, and we both laughed. "Is getting up early a habit with you?"

"Actually, sometimes." His hand stole up to take a lock of my hair. "In a big family, that's really the only time there's any quiet. I used to get up to run before I helped my dad in the shop."

"I was never a morning person," I said, "but I am now, so I know what you mean. It's the only time I can get stuff done."

We drove twenty minutes and arrived at a park near the entrance to one of the Camelback Mountain trails. "I knew we wouldn't have time to hike," he said as he parked.

"Already getting a little light," I agreed, pulling up

the hood of my jacket for added warmth over my mostly dry hair.

"Next time."

The comment sent a fluttering through my stomach, reminding me of last night's world-stopping kiss. I still wasn't sure what he saw in me, but I was glad that he did.

Dew marked the table, and Jameson made a face. "Didn't think of that, but I have a table cloth."

"I have something." I dug in my shoulder bag for the small pack of wipes I'd learned to carry in my purse since Ruth and Halla had come to live with me. You never knew when it would come in handy.

Instead of closing around the wipes, my hand met a block of cold. Puzzled, I drew it out to see one of the blue ice packs we'd used with Zoey and Bianca's lunches before they qualified for the free meals at school. "Elsie," I murmured. I hadn't seen her up, but it had to have been her, making sure I had ice for my very hot date.

"What's that?" Jameson asked.

I held up the ice pack. "Apparently, the girls think you're hot, so Elsie is making sure I have ice."

He laughed. "I'll have to thank them."

"They are definitely on your side." I put the blue rectangle back into my bag and found the wipes, wondering if the girls were a good judge of character, or if we were all setting ourselves up for some kind of letdown. Mario Jameson Perez was a man, after all, not some rich hero who would ride in on his white horse to save us.

Jameson's hand touched the sleeve of my jacket. "What is it?"

I sighed, pursing my lips. "It's just, even after all they've been through, they're still trusting, and sometimes—okay, all the time—I worry about letting them down."

"But you are doing *something*," he said. "Don't forget that. That's more than the rest of the world."

"Right. Look at the positive."

We wiped down the bench and much of the table, barely finishing in time to watch the sunrise. Fingers of light reflected from the beaded dew on the grass and trees. Jameson put his arm around me, and a peace settled over me.

My stomach chose that moment to remind us about the food.

"I hope you like eggs and bacon." Jameson hurried to open his picnic basket and pulled out round biscuits filled with still-warm eggs and several half strips of bacon.

There were no wrappers, so I had to ask, "Is there a deli open this early?"

"These I actually made. The biscuits are even fresh."

"I'm impressed."

"Well, don't be. It takes like ten minutes."

He still got up early to do it. I took a bite. "Mmm. I can't remember the last time anyone made me breakfast."

"Since you left home?"

I smiled and swallowed another bite before answering. "My mother doesn't make breakfast. Neither did my father. We had a housekeeper who made sure they had their omelets, or whatever, but my sister and I grew up on cold cereal."

"Like most of America, huh?" We ate for a few moments in easy silence, and then he said, "When did you decide to start helping girls? Was it when you found Saffron? I heard them say she's been with you the longest."

"Of the girls I have now, yeah. Saffron's been with me since last September. But I had two other girls on and off the year before that. They were older, though, students at my college who were having family problems. But it really all began when I was six."

"Six?" He laughed and shook his head. "Don't tell me. I can just see you sneaking a kid into your room. From what little you've said about your parents, you'd have to be pretty brave to do something like that."

I didn't think I'd told him anything about my parents, but we had talked a lot about other things, and I guess the relationship we didn't have showed through. "Actually, sneaking something into my room was much later, and it was a cat."

"So what happened when you were six?"

I gnawed on my lower lip, wondering how much to tell him. "I missed two months of my kindergarten year. I was really sick, and my mother hated the idea of me being behind because 'that's not what Crawfords do.'" I made quote marks with my finger to show they were her words, not mine. "So when I was better, instead of putting me into school, she sent me back to my old preschool, where I was bored enough that I started helping out with all the kids—getting the drinks, playing with the sad ones. That sort of thing. After I finally got to kindergarten, I just kept it up. I didn't like it when they left people out."

"I can believe it. And the cat?"

"I was seven, and I found a kitten someone had abandoned in a field. Little tiny thing." I showed him with my hands. "I had to feed her with an eyedropper. I had her hidden in my room for a week before my sister found out and three months before our parents discovered it."

"Resourceful." Jameson pushed the container of biscuits toward me. "No wonder you're good with the girls."

"Well, hopefully, with your help, I can do more. But we'd better get back. I need to drive the girls to school, and Ruth and Halla have some errands they're doing for people today, so I need to drop them off as well."

We cleaned up our picnic and walked back to the car. His fingers closed over mine. "Thanks for coming."

"Thank you for asking."

We reached the car, and he leaned over to kiss me. The kiss was so brief and chaste that my heart had no reason at all to be threatening to pound out of my chest or for my knees to lose all function. I sank gratefully into the seat as he opened the door, my hand going inside my bag to touch Elsie's ice pack.

It had only been two days, and I couldn't possibly be falling in love, but there was so much right about this man, and all my responsibilities hadn't scared him off yet. That alone was a miracle.

After her first few weeks with me, Saffron had started walking dogs, running errands, and cleaning for several widows at the church we attended. It had been her way of helping me buy our food—and to appease my roommates, who were at that time mostly too busy to notice I had a continuous, non-authorized visitor in my private room. When they did notice, they were never above eating our bribes.

Later when Ruth and Halla joined us, Saffron moved on to the burger place and passed her old jobs onto them. Since both Ruth and Halla had poor social skills and dressed funny, it was unlikely they would have convinced strangers to trust them without Saffron's hearty recommendation, so it worked out perfectly. It had taken encouragement in the beginning, and many times I'd been late to class to go with them, but now the girls were reliable, and the widows loved them. They had regular clients on Tuesdays, Thursdays, and Saturdays. The errands didn't pay a lot, but the income helped them buy clothes, food, and other necessities my income wouldn't stretch enough to cover.

Unfortunately, their first job was far enough away that they needed me to drive them if they were ever to arrive on time—they were still young girls and liked their sleep. From the first widow's house, they'd go from job to job until they arrived home.

"What about Elsie?" Ruth asked as we climbed into my car.

"Saffron is staying with her." I hoped I'd remembered to put everything in my binder. I'd brought the court papers for Zoey and Bianca, but they were the only girls I was willing to talk about to Jameson's friend. Maybe I'd add Ruth, eventually, because her mother didn't seem to want her home, but I needed to find out what I had to do to be qualified. I couldn't let any of the girls return to dangerous situations.

As I dropped the girls off, making sure they had their lunches and money for an emergency phone call, I worried about the meeting. What if Zoey and Bianca's uncle changed his mind and wanted them back? Maybe this wasn't such a great idea. Still, I decided to go to the meeting because if I didn't change something, I didn't know how we could ever do more than simply survive.

Teen Remake was located in a corner office in downtown Phoenix, next to a dentist and a chiropractor. The front office even looked like a dentist's office, down to the young receptionist, who looked up from behind a desk when I walked in. "May I help you?"

"I'm Lily Crawford. I'm here for a meeting about becoming licensed as a foster parent?"

"Oh, Mario's friend." Her smile put me at ease. "Sure, the interview."

What she meant by that wasn't exactly clear, but I was glad I hadn't mentioned Jameson by name, or she would have wondered. I might have to rethink the name choice.

"Yeah, is he here?"

The words were barely out of my mouth when he came through the open door. "Hi, Lily, come on back." He held out a beckoning hand.

The receptionist gave me a nod and turned her sweet smile to a stressed-looking couple who had come in the door after me. They were probably here about their child.

"What exactly does Teen Remake do?" I asked in a low voice as Jameson's hand touched my back, leading me though the door. "It's not one of those boot camp behavioral places, is it? Where parents ship off their kids and don't see them for months? I've heard terrible things about those."

"No, we're not like that. Well, we do take the kids camping, but it's not abusive or threatening the way some programs are. Parents are always invited, and why not? In most cases, they're the ones paying for the treatment. Basically, what Teen Remake does is to figure out what's gone wrong in the child's life and try to remake that part so the rest can work as it should. The first step is understanding why the teens don't want to do whatever it is their parents and society requires of them. It involves a lot of talking and activities, and that's why we use not only paid counselors, but a lot of volunteers. For the most part, the children are still living at home or in foster homes, so we don't have children staying here, though we do have connections with a group home we sometimes send them to." Jameson's face had become animated, telling me how much he enjoyed his work.

"A lot of the time, we're working with the parents just as much as the kids," he added, lowering his voice, even though we were far enough away from the front now that no one could overhear. "Frankly, there are far too many instances where parents simply expect too much too fast from kids. We find that easing the expectations, without abandoning them all together, of course, helps them show the child the love they really need. Teaching the parents to moderate their responses and to take time to think about their actions helps everyone."

"You sound like you really love it."

We rounded a bend in the hall. "I do. I've seen kids completely change. Of course, the really violent ones or those with severe addictions aren't referred to us. But we do get a lot of kids with depression, kids who cut themselves, refuse to do homework, sneak out at night, steal stuff. That sort of thing."

Half of this new hallway was full of windows, allowing us to see into the rooms. In one, young teens sat in a circle, throwing a ball. In another, they were playing video games. "I know what you're thinking," Jameson said. "But those video games are specifically designed for depression. It's a pilot program."

"The girls and I play games quite a bit on the weekends." I hesitated before adding, "Zoey still cuts herself sometimes, but a lot less than she used to."

"Well, if we get you approved, maybe she can come here. She'd probably do really well because our programs are hands-on instead of bookwork or lectures."

"I'll be interested to see more."

"Oh, you're going to love it." He paused in front of a door. The window on this room had shutters that were angled upward, obscuring most of the inside. "Here we are. Bea, the woman you're seeing today, is a counselor with the Department of Child Safety, or DCS as we call it, and she comes in part-time each week to check on the progress of the children they've sent to us whose programs the state is subsidizing."

He reached for the door as he added, "I talked to Bea this morning when I arrived and gave her the heads up on Zoey and Bianca."

Unexpected anger made me catch my breath. I'd wanted to test out the woman first, to see how I felt about her. Now there was no going back.

Jameson tapped on the door. "Come in," called a voice.

We went inside, and the woman behind the desk stood up to greet us. She was probably in her late thirties, but it was hard to tell by the ebony smoothness of her skin. Her hair was as dark as Ruth's frizzy mess, but it was gelled and conditioned and scrunched to a beautiful perfection. I'd researched this style for African-American women and had tried it on Ruth in the hope of getting her to lose the hat, but we hadn't been all that successful. Maybe it was time to try again, because this woman's hair was amazing.

She came around the desk, her slim hand extended. "Hi, I'm Bea Lundberg. I'm a social worker with the Department of Child Safety, but I also provide oversight here at Teen Remake. You must be Lily. Nice to meet you."

"Nice to meet you too."

"Please have a seat."

I glanced at Jameson, who nodded and thumbed at the door. "I have to get back to work. Check in with me before you leave?"

I felt a slight panic, but I pushed it away. Of course he had to work. "You just want to play video games."

"Busted. I could get someone else to fill in for me, if you'd—"

"No, no, I'm good." It was better this way because he'd met all the girls, and I didn't want him slipping. He'd already said more than enough. I gave him a wave and sat down in the nearest of the three seats Bea had indicated in front of the desk.

Instead of returning to sit behind her desk, Bea sat

down next to me, tugging down her pencil skirt and crossing her legs. "So, Mario tells me you have a few girls living with you, and you're interested in becoming their official foster parent."

"Well, I'm already their guardian, but it's basically for school purposes." I drew out the papers from my binder and handed them to her. "The judge was clear that it didn't mean I had custody."

"Yeah, there's a lot more involved for that." Her eyes skimmed the papers briefly. "Tell me about the girls."

I told her about their mother dying and how they'd gone to their uncle's to live, where they'd stayed for two years before finally running away in December. "I found them in a park. I usually go to Flagstaff over the Christmas break, but luckily, I stayed."

My mother had been livid at that, but I hadn't dared leave Saffron, Ruth, and Halla for more than one day. It would have been different if my mother had been the kind to open her home to visitors. Saffron, she might have welcomed, thinking she was a roommate, but not Ruth or Halla.

"They were sleeping at the park?"

"Not until right before I found them. They'd been staying with different friends, but it was the day after Christmas, and I guess they ran out of places to go."

Ruth had seen them first on Christmas afternoon when I'd been at my parents' during the day, and we'd gone looking for them when I returned to Phoenix, but they must have hidden. I'd gone back the next morning, just to be sure, and found them cold and unhappy.

"Bianca was crying, and they were both hungry and

needed baths," I said. "It didn't take much to convince them to come home with me. Later, I talked to their uncle, and he agreed to let them stay."

"Just like that?" Bea's raised eyebrow implied doubt.

I met her gaze. "I told him I knew he'd been abusing Zoey sexually and had started on Bianca. That's why Zoey ran and took Bianca with her. She didn't want her sister to be abused like she'd been."

Bea's lips tightened. "Poor kids. And the uncle's given you no money?"

"No. I was able to get the girls free lunches, though, using my income and the guardianship papers."

"Good." Bea uncrossed her leg and leaned forward. "The first thing that needs to happen here is I need to talk to Zoey and Bianca. I can do that at their school, if it's more convenient. Then I'll go visit their uncle as a precursor to getting you some funds for their care."

"He won't pay," I said. "As he said to me, they're not even his kids."

"Since he's not the birth parent, it's unlikely he'd be charged maintenance anyway, unless there was an inheritance he received when the girls' mother died. Or unless he wanted to work toward keeping custody."

I took a deep breath before saying, "That can't happen. Zoey was also abused by at least three of his friends. She's pretty sure they paid her uncle."

Bea's nostrils flared, hinting that she was as upset as I was about Zoey's situation. "Not the first time I've seen that. At any rate, because he's already assigned guardianship to you, we're almost there. We just need the state to take custody."

"I don't want to do anything if that means they'll be uprooted again. Not even for help. They're happy now."

Her eyes bore into mine. "I'm good at what I do, and that is helping children like Zoey and Bianca. I believe from what Mario told me that they're in a good situation now, and since you mentioned sexual abuse, I am required to conduct a thorough investigation. Even if their uncle wants them, they won't be returned to him any time soon, as long as both girls are claiming abuse."

I believed her, but she didn't know how I'd threatened him into signing. Would he tell her? And there was still the other side of the issue—whether or not they'd stay with me. I'd heard horror stories about some foster homes. "Look, I know you mean well, but I've heard of so many times where kids keep being sent back into situations that turn out to be dangerous. I just don't want that to happen to them."

"It's true kids fall into the cracks. I've seen parents lie like crazy to get their children back, fooling everyone but the child, and I've seen social workers who are too overworked to see through the lies or to check up as often as they should. I've even seen children who die before we can help them. But that's not going to happen here. These girls have you to fight for them. And now they have me."

On the surface, her comments were great for Zoey and Bianca, but they were also one more reason not to tell her about the other girls. I wasn't willing to risk their lives, especially when Halla had barely escaped her father, and I still had no idea what Elsie had been through. "I'm not sure I can even pass any tests that DCS might require."

Bea leaned back again with a little sigh. "Fortunately—or unfortunately in some cases—that's the easy part. It takes about thirty hours of training, but almost anyone can qualify to be a foster parent. And that's why you're here, right? To get licensed and learn how you can help the girls—though from what Mario has told me, you are probably a step ahead of most potential foster parents in terms of experience."

My stomach clenched as I wondered what else he'd said, but asking would look suspicious. "But I'm single, and my apartment isn't the best."

She shook her head. "That might factor in with young children or children in high demand, but two Hispanic teenagers who want to be placed together aren't going to be at the top of anyone's list. As long as they have a place to sleep and food and a bathroom, and it's not too crowded, it'll be fine. We will have to do an onsite check, of course."

That's what I was afraid of. Seven girls in a one-bedroom apartment was probably far too many, though we could clean up the fold-out chair beds and hide the other girls during the visit.

Bea must have read something in my face that told her I was okay with her suggestion. "First let me get the ball rolling with the uncle. Until the state takes custody, there is no issue about the girls staying with you. Your guardianship papers give you all you need. So if you'll give me their school information, I can drop by and chat with them. It'll facilitate things if you call the school to let them know."

"I can do that." No doubt she wanted to talk to them

about staying with me, and that didn't worry me. They wouldn't talk about the other girls.

"While I'm working it all out, you can concentrate on getting licensed."

"Okay." With the decision made, the tension in my gut eased.

"So, is there anything else you'd like to discuss?"

My heart lodged somewhere in my throat. Just how much had Jameson told her? Had he hinted about the other girls? I was so going to kill him. As soon as I had the chance. For now, I needed to answer the social worker, but already my delay would have told her I was hiding something.

Slowly, I shook my head. "Nothing you can help with." That much was true. "I do have another girl living with me, but she's almost eighteen, and she already passed the GED. Her parents kicked her out about a year ago. Her birthday is in less than two months, and she's very in charge of her own life. She has no desire to see her parents or get involved with the state." I smiled and added, "But I'll ask her."

Bea studied me for a few seconds before nodding. "Fair enough. You're probably right on all accounts—as long as she's not technically a runaway with someone looking for her. Anyway, if she's working and has a place to stay, a judge would probably emancipate her. Not all seventeen-year-olds are that independent."

Saffron hadn't been either, not when I'd found her. But she was resilient, and she'd come back. She'd learned from her mistakes.

"I'm glad she has you," Bea added.

I hoped she was sincere and wouldn't show up at the apartment to harass Saffron. At least I hadn't given her my address, and the court papers listed my previous residence. I hadn't gotten around to changing the school records either, and I wouldn't do it until I was sure how things would go with Zoey and Bianca.

Bea stood and waved the guardianship papers. "Is it okay if I take a copy of these?"

"Yes."

"Come with me, then. I'll show you where the copy center is." She laughed as she waited for me to go through the door. "Actually, it's a glorified name for a closet with a copy machine in it. But you may need to make copies for activities, so I might as well show you now."

Huh? I followed her out, my brain scrambling to keep up.

"Did Mario tell you that the job requires one evening a week?" Bea looked at me as we walked down the hall.

"He didn't say."

"Is that going to be a problem with the girls? They're old enough for you to leave for one evening, I think. Or do you have someone who could stay with them?"

I stopped walking. "I'm not even sure what you're talking about. Is that what's required for the license?"

She laughed. "Goodness no. I'm talking about a job here at Teen Remake, especially working with our Teens Back to Nature camping program, or Teen Nature for short. I thought you were also here to interview for one of the part-time jobs we have open, but if you're not interested . . ."

An image of my job at the cereal factory flashed

through my mind. Hair nets and gloves and bits of cereal in my eyes. Machines humming, standing for hours in the same place, reports and more reports. And looming over everything, my father's expectations.

"Oh, I'm interested," I said quickly. "I have another job, but it's only part time so I could finish college, and I need full time work now."

I was actually still on my college work schedule: four hours on Mondays and Wednesdays, and six hours on Tuesdays and Thursdays. "I can possibly adjust my schedule there, and I have a friend who can stay with the girls, if needed."

Bea held out her hand. "Then welcome to the team. You'll still have to meet with the director here to talk about a schedule, but he often has me screen his applicants, so I don't anticipate any issues. He's actually meeting with some parents this morning, or he'd have been in on this meeting."

"This is because of the girls, isn't it? That you're offering me the job."

Her smile widened. "Partially, yes, but also because Mario recommends you so highly. After meeting you, I have to agree that you'll be great. Half the boys are going to fall in love with you, and half the girls will want to be just like you. Plus, you look like someone the parents will trust. You can do a lot of good here, Lily. We do have a lot of applicants every year, but it's hard to find people we know will be good."

"Don't the kids have school? How are you even open during the week?"

"Most attend school, but our programs count for

credit, so the kids come here a few times a week like they do for regular classes. There are those who can't function yet in a regular school, and we have extended programs for them. Teen Nature currently runs from Thursday morning to Saturday night, so they only miss two school days for the camping experience. Kids can participate once every two months, and it has to be approved by their regular teachers, and usually they get credit toward an assignment. The camps are really fun, so most of the kids try hard to make it. When school lets out for the summer, we'll hold longer camps."

One evening a week? I could do that, and having a foot in the door would only help me with the battles I still had ahead for Elsie, Ruth, and Halla. The extra money might mean we could afford a better apartment.

I was still upset at Jameson for telling Bea about Zoey and Bianca before I had the chance to check her out, but I was grateful too. Trusting him did seem to be taking me in the right direction.

Bea showed me the copy machine and how to work it. Then she took me to several of the rooms and introduced me to the teens who crowded around us. They liked Bea, and that made me feel excited for what she could do to help my situation.

We found Jameson in one of the rooms with five teenage boys. They were no longer playing video games, but tossing a foam basketball into a hoop. They waved lazily as they saw us coming. Jameson hurried toward the door, a welcoming smile on his face.

Bea nudged me and whispered, "Remember what I said about the boys falling in love? Looks like one of them is already halfway there."

6

When I arrived home from work that evening after a grueling six-hour shift, I was surprised to see Ruth running down to the parking lot to meet me. "Someone came by earlier," she said as we climbed up the stairs. "A woman. I didn't open the door, of course."

"What did she look like?"

"White woman with blond hair. Older, real pretty. Rich-looking."

So not Bea Lundberg. Of course, it couldn't have been, unless Jameson had given her my address, because on Teen Remake's employee papers, I'd listed Tessa's, just in case. "Did she say anything? Leave a note on the door?"

"No, she just rang and left. She did seem kind of familiar, though. Not sure where I saw her before."

"Did she look like Saffron or Halla?" I was going to get a stomach ulcer with all the worry.

"No. I don't think so. Maybe."

"Well, you did the right thing. Hopefully soon, we won't have to worry. I talked to a social worker today."

We'd reached the landing on the fourth floor, and Ruth stopped walking, her brow furrowing. "About me?"

"No, honey." I put my arm around her. She was getting so tall that she'd already passed me by an inch. When had that happened? And her body was much thinner than all the clothes led one to believe. "About Zoey and Bianca. I'm going to get licensed as a foster parent, so I can officially have them as my foster kids. Once that happens, I'll go talk to your mother and feel her out."

Ruth's brow furrowed and her dark eyes looked sad. "She ain't gonna sign any papers. Not if she's still living with that white piece of trash. *He* wants me there."

"Don't worry. That's not going to happen. And I don't plan on talking to him."

"I know." But she frowned as she glanced over my shoulder at the vehicle that was pulling into the lot below. "Hey, isn't that Mario's car?"

Sure enough, it was. "He texted me about stopping by, but I'm surprised he's here already."

His text had acted on me like a huge dose of caffeine, pushing away the tiredness I'd felt for the past two hours. There'd been no time for private talk at Teen Remake before I left for work, and I was eager to have it out with him, or give him a hug. I wasn't sure which.

Ruth grinned at my expression. "Maybe he wants to go out with you again."

"I've got to help Bianca with a report."

"Too bad. He is fine on the eyes, I'll say that much," Ruth murmured as we waited for him to join us.

I rolled my eyes, however right she was. "How did work go today?"

"Good, but that Mrs. Jenkins' poodle seriously needs an attitude adjustment. Halla had to rescue him from a big dog this morning that was finally sick of his yapping." She giggled. "You should have seen it. That teeny, tiny rat of a dog, going after a big black lab, or whatever he was. We're just glad the rat can't talk or the spoiled little thing would probably tattle on us for not letting him do what he wants, and then we'd get fired."

I laughed, but all my attention was on Jameson now, who was coming up the final flight of steps. His grin answered mine as he saw me. He looked good for having spent an entire day at work. Really good. Though at some point he'd changed from the dress slacks and polo to worn jeans and a T-shirt that had seen better days.

"So," I said. "What's up? Your text was kind of cryptic." Was it too soon to hope he'd ask me out again?

He reached into a canvas bag he was carrying and pulled out a tool belt. "I thought I'd fix your cupboard, if you don't mind."

"Our cupboard?" I stared at him blankly.

He glanced at Ruth, who grimaced. "Uh, yeah," she said. "Been meaning to tell you about that. The other day, Halla and I got messing around in the kitchen, and that cupboard where you keep the extra canned food? Well, it sort of . . . came off."

I counted to ten before I responded. I'd lost track of the times I'd told them to stop horsing around in that tiny kitchen. But really, it wasn't their fault—there wasn't much room and nowhere for them to play or to work off their energy. "When was this? I haven't noticed anything."

"It was Tuesday when you were at work. Halla and I taped the hinge, but it came off when Mario was helping me wash dishes yesterday."

"I see."

"You're not mad, are you?" Ruth gave me a puppy dog look.

"No, but next time tell me. It's better to fix it before it gets worse." Besides, there was no way I could be upset when it meant I got to see Jameson again for the third time today. Still, I didn't want him to think he had to be taking care of us all the time. We'd been doing fine before he showed up.

Then again, the world had moved when he'd kissed me—and that hadn't ever happened that I could remember. Shooting him a quick glance, I saw that he was watching me with a grin that turned my stomach to mush.

"They make these places as cheap as they can," he said. "But it won't take long to fix. The screws have just stripped the channel they're in. I'll put in some wood putty and tomorrow we can screw it back in. Good as new. Or better, probably."

"Well, thank you." I led them to the apartment, where Ruth had left the door slightly ajar. That made me nervous with Elsie so concerned about being found, but I'd talk to Ruth about it later.

All the girls were home, except Saffron, who had sent me a text about a hot date that she promised to keep at arm's length. I knew she meant it; she'd learned a hard lesson that was still fresh, and she'd gone through five guys in just the last month because they demanded more than she was ready to give. I was proud of her for that.

While Jameson went to work removing the cupboard door, I went to check on Elsie, who was reading, and then started Bianca on her paper, letting her use my laptop that was normally off limits when I wasn't home to supervise.

"Well, everyone, listen up," I said, finally joining Jameson in the kitchen. "I have an announcement to make." I waited until the girls looked at me or clustered around, even Elsie, who'd decided to emerge from the bedroom. "I am now working part time at Teen Remake, mostly for their camping program, but also one half day each week at their regular offices. The only catch is I have to be away one evening a week. That means I'll work noon to ten on Fridays."

A disappointed chorus of "Aaaaaw" met my announcement.

"Don't worry," I said. "We'll switch our movie night to Saturday. I also have to work four hours Thursday and Saturday mornings, to get in the eighteen hours they're allowing me, but it'll be a lot more money coming in overall. I don't begin until next week."

The girls were satisfied with that and became more excited when I told them about Bea and training to be a foster parent. "But for the record," Zoey said, "if it doesn't work out, we're running away again."

"It'll work out," I assured her.

Zoey and Halla wandered back to the living room where Bianca was tapping on my computer. Elsie and Ruth stayed close. "Maybe your house dream is going to come true," Elsie said, low enough for only me to hear. I smiled at her.

"What about your other job?" Jameson asked from where he knelt on the floor with his screwdriver.

I shrugged. "There is some job security being the boss's

daughter, even if he's not exactly happy with my choice of degree, but the days don't overlap except on Thursdays. I get off at Teen Remake at noon and have until one to get to the factory. I will have to drop off Ruth and Halla at their jobs a little sooner on Thursdays, or have my sister do it."

"I'm good with that," Ruth said, settling at the small round table, a book in hand. "Tessa's nice."

I was more worried about what to do with Elsie on Thursdays. I'd have four hours at Teen Remake, training hours that hadn't been optional, and six at the factory. Saffron would be working by then, and with the other girls gone most of the day doing errands for their older ladies, Elsie would be alone. Twelve was plenty old enough to stay by herself, but she wasn't just any twelve-year-old, and I didn't like it.

Maybe Makay would have room in her schedule to pop in and check on her. Or Ruth and Halla could take her along on their jobs. Or if things worked out with the foster parenting and Teen Remake, I could cut Thursday afternoons at the factory altogether. I'd do that in a heart-beat, but not until I had another way to pay for food and rent.

Jameson began stuffing putty inside the stripped holes. I'd fixed another cupboard once before using paper glue and the ends of a couple matchsticks—a tip I'd read about in a novel—but this certainly looked more professional, though once the hinge was back on, no one would see it. Finally satisfied, he stood the cupboard door up against the wall to dry and put his spatula back in his tool belt, now around his waist. There was something compelling about him in those old jeans and that belt. Sexy and manly. It was so cliché I had to roll my eyes at myself.

"What," he said, sounding slightly offended.

"Nothing." I turned away and started looking through the other cupboards, hoping to hide the color flushing my face. "Guess we need to find something for dinner."

"I'll be heading out, then," he said, still with that wounded tone.

I didn't want him going away offended. "You could stay." The words were out before I could stop them. I'd only just met him, and I didn't want to push things any faster than I already had. I quickly resolved to be less eager.

His grin melted my resolve to a warm puddle of contentment. "I'd love to," he said, "but I have to grab a shower before I head to South Mountain. A Teen Nature group went out this morning, and I'm doing a campfire activity for them." He laughed. "Actually, it's more of making an idiot of myself. The kids get a real kick out of it."

"Oh, I can imagine. So do you always help out with Teen Nature?"

"Yeah, at least one day a week, but I've asked to switch to Fridays." He gave me a wink that made me wish for Elsie's ice pack. Guess my asking him to stay had smoothed over the awkwardness between us.

The doorbell ringing saved me from responding. Ruth jumped up from the table where she was examining the repaired hole in the cupboard and hurried to the door. Everyone else froze. Elsie grabbed my hand.

"It's okay," I murmured.

"It's that woman again," Ruth said in a whisper that carried through the apartment.

"Do we need to go up on the roof?" Elsie asked, pressing herself against me.

"No." I glanced at Jameson and saw him frowning at Elsie, and I knew her fear bothered him. I hated it too.

Ruth stepped back as I hurried to look through the peephole. The older woman standing there was blond and beautiful and well-dressed. Her hair swept up into a stylish twist in the back, and her trim suit and high heels looked completely out of place here.

I had no idea how she'd found me. "It's my mother," I said. A collective sigh of relief ran through the room. Only I remained tense.

Ruth snapped her fingers. "Right, she looks like you! That's why she's familiar."

There might be a family resemblance, but after working at the factory and being up since four, I looked more like her scraggly stepchild. For a moment, I was tempted to not open the door at all, but if she'd tracked me here, she'd be back. Nothing left to do but face her.

Taking a breath, I opened the door six inches, placing myself in the space so she didn't have much of a view inside. Ruth started to come around the door to peer out, but I shook my head, and she retreated into the kitchen.

"Mother! What a surprise."

She gave a delicate snort. "I'll bet. Why didn't you tell me you were moving? I went to your old place, and your roommate, that nice dark-haired girl—Brette, I think she said her name was—told me you'd moved here." Her lips pursed as she tried to see past me, where everything was still quiet.

"She knew the apartment number? That's good." And unlikely. Brette Silvan had been my only supportive roommate, and she'd helped us move, but I hadn't seen her since, and I doubted she remembered which apartment I was in.

"Well, I did have to knock on the manager's door here and talk with him." Her nose wrinkled. "He told me the number."

"Haven't you heard of texting?" I kept my tone light because that was the best way to deal with my mother.

"Oh, darling, texting is so . . . so tedious. I called but you didn't answer. I left a message."

Now that she mentioned it, I vaguely remembered seeing my message light blinking, but the calls had come when I was at work on the line, and it was impossible to answer then. Once I'd seen Jameson's text, I'd forgotten everything else. Not very smart since the call could have come from the girls.

She gazed around the outdoor hallway, and for a moment I saw the chipped and stained cement, the dusty old brick, and the flimsy black railing that was scraped in more than a few spots. "You *live* here? This really isn't—"

"It's not so bad," I said brightly. "Was there something you wanted to tell me? Or were you just in town?"

"Lily." Her voice showed disapproval. "The management at your previous apartment told me you had unauthorized visitors. That your roommates complained."

Each statement was an accusation. "What's going on? I talked to Tessa only a few days ago, and she didn't mention you'd moved."

"Yeah, it happened so fast. I didn't have the chance to tell her." No way was I dragging Tessa into this. Next, our mother would be asking her to keep an eye on me and report any bad behavior.

"Well, aren't you going to invite me in? It's getting dark, and I don't think it's quite safe out here."

"Now isn't really a good time."

"Lily, I've driven all this way."

Now that she was here, there was no stopping her. I sighed internally and stepped away from the door. Inside, everyone watched my mother uneasily, except Elsie, who was probably hiding in the bedroom again.

"Oh, I didn't know you had company." My mother's eyes fell over the girls and stopped on Jameson.

He nodded at her and then looked expectantly at me. I so did *not* want to introduce him. Not in a million years. Especially with that tool belt on. I knew my mother would never think him worthy of my notice with that tool belt. "This is my mother," I announced unnecessarily. "Mom, these are my roommates."

Her eyes widened and went to Jameson again. I felt a sneaking gratification at her reaction.

"Not me," Jameson said quickly. He checked his hand and came toward us as he extended it, "Hi, I'm Mario Perez, Lily's friend. Nice to meet you."

My mother shook his hand gingerly. "You too." If her voice was any stiffer, it'd break.

To me, he added, "I'd better go."

"Thanks for fixing the cupboard."

At that, my mother relaxed, and the little girl inside me who had seen her drop my rescued cat off at the pound felt both saddened and angry. I *liked* Jameson, and I didn't care if my mother thought he was a blue-collar worker with no future. Money could help dreams come true, but it couldn't create them, and there was a whole lot more out there that was more important than rich friends and the right silverware.

"I'll see you tomorrow night?" I asked Jameson. Or maybe the little girl inside me asked.

His dark eyes actually gleamed, completely blotting out my mother's disapproval. "Of course. Looking forward to it."

Our gazes caught and held, and I knew that if my mother and the girls weren't around, we'd be doing a whole lot more kissing and a lot less staring. I wet my lip with my tongue and saw his eyes follow the motion. Suddenly, I couldn't wait to be alone with him. "I'll walk you down."

His grin widened. "That's okay. I wouldn't want to interrupt your chat with your mother." With another nod to her and the girls, he strode through the door, radiating so much power and confidence that even my mother stared, and leaving me feeling . . . what, I didn't know for sure, but it might be a little bit of pride.

When I turned from shutting the door, I found my mother watching me, her arms folded. That was how it was with her—hands not on her hips but tucked under her arms as if holding herself apart from the world. From me and Tessa.

"I was just about to make some dinner," I said. "Want to help?"

"Are you dating him?" There it was, the condescension I'd heard her use when talking about the boy at the car wash who'd hit on me senior year, or whenever she signed a package for the UPS guy.

"Yes," I said. One date didn't mean we were dating, but I wanted it to.

"Is he Mexican?"

How did I know that was coming? She had him weighed and judged, if not in the instant she'd stepped into the room, then certainly from the moment he told her his name. I glanced at the girls in the living room, but they didn't appear to be paying attention to either of us. Only Ruth was close enough to hear the intended slur, but she was deep in a book.

"I'm not sure his ethnicity matters. Look, Mom, he's a nice guy, and I like him." I wanted to tell her about his family coming from Spain, about his plans for an MBA, and how he worked at Teen Remake, but at the last second, I couldn't force the words past my lips. She'd already made up her mind, and my answers to her inevitable questions about his roots and his father's employment would likely send us both over the top.

She sighed. "You need to come home."

A sudden intake of breath told me Ruth wasn't as occupied with her book as she pretended.

"Actually, what I need is to make dinner. It's my night." I forced a bit of apology into my voice. "But I'd love to get together another day."

My mother looked from me to Ruth, to the other girls

in the living room. She was smart enough to notice that most of them weren't anywhere near eighteen. But she didn't call me on it.

Instead, she cracked a partial smile. "Your father is thinking about opening an overseas factory. You were always good at languages, so that might be right up your alley. If you could work in some French classes next semester."

There it was, as I'd known it would be. It always came down to my mother placing me to her advantage, or in this case the factory's. And of course, French would be the language of her choice, because in her mind it represented romance, society, and culture.

The exhaustion I'd been fighting came rushing back like water closing over my head. "That's a good idea. Thanks for letting me know."

Her smile was real this time because she'd said what she'd come here to say, and I'd listened. "You will be coming for the Fourth, right? It's just around the corner. We'll stake out a place for the parade, of course. I'm inviting some friends. I'm so excited to show you and Tessa off."

"I'll be there." Oddly enough, the event was the one thing we did that gave me a sense of family. I didn't know if that was because I loved the park where we picnicked after the parade, or because my mom would always invite some other family and I enjoyed the peek into their lives, especially if they seemed more normal than our family. At any rate, my parents were always on their best behavior for the day. No arguing or irritation or isolating silences. We played at being the average family.

"Well, I'll be going." She held out her arms for a hug, which I allowed. "You really should do something with your hair," she whispered, fluffing it as she drew away. "I have some deep conditioning I'll send you."

"It's just from the hairnets at work." But I didn't refuse her offer. The conditioner might be good for Ruth or even Elsie, if the child would ever let me fix her hair. I opened the door. "Thanks for the visit, Mom. I'll walk you out."

She smiled. "Thank you, dear."

On the way down the stairs, we passed my second-floor neighbor with his ever-present cigarette between two fingers, his unshaven face contrasting with his new-looking jeans and black dress shirt. He had dark eyes most women would call sexy, but I thought they were calculating, and the way his long hair fell into his face made me think of a teenager. He watched us unblinking as we passed, with no emotion and not even the barest nod of his head. He'd hit on me the first week we'd been here, and since I'd refused a date, he hadn't so much as cracked a smile.

My mother glanced back at him after we had passed. "I don't like you being here with his kind."

She was right about him, so I couldn't object, but she had to add as we arrived at her white Lexus, "It was good to see you, but please remember what I said about that man in your apartment. He isn't from our circle. You need to look for men who have a similar status to your own."

The ridiculousness of it made me laugh. "I don't have any status. I haven't even graduated from college. I work part-time at a cereal factory, and I live in a dump." Not to mention that Jameson's major was the exact same one my parents had tried to push on me. I didn't fool myself that even a finished MBA would be enough to endear him to them, unless he had a rich relative I didn't know about.

"You work as a line manager at your *father's* successful factory." Her voice was full of sharp points and angles. "And you had a perfectly respectable apartment—which, I might add, you paid for with the very generous wage we give you for your work at the factory. You would still have that nice apartment if you didn't collect stray girls like cats. You also have a perfectly wonderful house to go home to."

"The girls aren't strays. They have me."

"You know that I have always believed in charity work, but this is a little extreme, don't you think? Organizations have been created to take care of these things, and the best thing we can do to help people in need is to support those organizations."

Organizations were my mother's specialty. She was good at raising money for charities, being on committees, and talking about how to improve things for the less fortunate. Good at it as long as it didn't sully her hands or her house—or, apparently, her daughters. We'd never even served dinner in a homeless shelter as a family.

"Well, someone's got to be in the trenches," I said. "Foster parents are the solution the organizations use to help kids."

"You should be focusing on finishing your education and launching your career."

"I will finish, but I am also the girls' guardian, and

I need to make sure they finish out the school year." I was hoping the half-truths would mollify her. Because the end of the school year wouldn't mean the end of my involvement, and I was only guardian to two of the girls. Lies by omission were what Tessa and I called these half-truths. My parents' house thrived on them.

My mother heaved a sigh, one hand resting on her open car door. "Lily, you can't help all of them. There are too many runaways and too many abuses in this world for one person to correct. You really aren't doing those girls a favor."

As if the pressure in my head were suddenly released, my anger faded. This woman, this "pretend" mother, had no comprehension of what I was doing, no understanding of the girls' needs, and she was separated from ever understanding by her money and her precious status. That meant she was forever excluded from knowing the joys of being involved. Not something to be angry over—it just made me very, very sad.

"Thanks for coming, Mom. I'll see you on the Fourth."

My neighbor was nowhere to be seen as I went back upstairs. The minute I walked into the apartment, Ruth popped out of the chair. "I don't know why we haven't met her before. She wasn't so bad."

"If you like ice queens," muttered Zoey from the couch.

I couldn't hide my smile.

"So, you know that you and Mario don't have plans tomorrow, right?" Halla added. "At least, you didn't tell us anything about a date."

"No, not a date. We'll both be at Teen Nature for my new work."

Ruth grinned. "I thought you said you don't start until next week, and he's going tonight. He only does one night a week, right?"

"Yep," Zoey said. "That means you made a date with him—we all heard you."

Now the gleam in Jameson's eyes made sense. He'd thought I was asking him out! I crossed the room and sank down on the couch, uncertain how I felt about that. I mean, I wanted to go out with him, but I didn't want to appear desperate or have him think I asked him because of my mother, which in a way, I guess I had.

"So where are you going to take him?" Bianca asked.

"I don't know." I could explain everything to him and he'd understand, but I hadn't imagined the attraction between us, and that meant dating him was a good idea. Even if I'd done the asking. "I'll let you know when I figure it out. For now, we need to finish your report."

Whatever I did with Jameson, I was sure there would be fireworks, and that made me all shivery inside. Shivery good.

I might just be falling for him.

Maybe.

F riday morning came early—probably because I'd been tossing and turning on the couch. Truthfully, I hadn't slept well since I'd moved to this apartment and had to sleep on the couch, and I was seriously considering using a pillow and blanket in the bathtub, or squeezing in with the girls in the bedroom. If they were really my sisters, that's what I'd do, but I didn't know how that would go over with DCS.

Halla took Zoey and Bianca to school, so I went back to sleep on Zoey and Bianca's double mattress for a half hour. I still needed to go see Payden at the grocery store, but I didn't have to work at the factory, which made me want to weep with joy. Just feeling that way made me depressed about going back on Monday.

Sometime later, I opened my eyes to see Elsie standing over me, her hands behind her back. "Oh, is it time?" My phone alarm hadn't buzzed yet.

"No, but . . ." She trailed off. "I was just . . . well, maybe I'll go with you to see Payden."

I smiled. "I'm sure he'd love that." I was just as sure she

had a crush on him. He was five years older, but he was socially a lot younger that most seventeen-year-olds, and I wasn't concerned. He'd been a good friend to both of us.

She brought out her hand and showed me a brush I recognized as mine from the bathroom. "I was going to ask . . . maybe could you comb my hair?"

Trying not to act excited, I stretched and sat up. "Sure, but we should probably start with washing and conditioning it. That might help." Ruth's detangler should work on Elsie's long hair.

Twenty minutes later, I was on the couch, combing out the strands. It wasn't as difficult as I'd expected, but still ten times more trying than my own. When we were finished, the difference was startling. She no longer looked like a street urchin. "You look beautiful," I said.

A darkness waved momentarily across her face, but she shook her head abruptly, as if shaking out an unwanted thought, and smiled shyly. "Thank you."

"Let's go."

I had no time to shower, of course, or put on makeup, but I wasn't trying to impress Payden. I dragged the brush through my hair as I waited at a traffic light.

"So, did you decide where to take Mario?" Elsie asked.

"Not yet."

"Maybe a movie?"

"Maybe."

Then because Jameson had told me how much time he spent with Payden since his father died, I pinched my cheeks and ran a tube of lipstick over my lips before getting out of the car. Just in case Jameson stopped by on a break or something.

Inside, we bought a small bag of Elsie's favorite chips, and Payden's face lit up when he saw her. By the time we got around to the back of the store, Payden was already there.

"Hey, Elsie," he said. "You look nice."

She shrugged and blushed. "Lily helped with my hair."

"It was a challenge, I tell you," I said. "She had like five rat nests. We had to evict all the tenants." Payden laughed, but Elsie's blush deepened, so I added, "Kidding, of course. She has great hair. What have we got here today?"

I took the box from his arms and pretended great interest while the two stared at each other without talking. Elsie wasn't usually this reticent and neither was Payden.

"So," I said, after a bit. "Maybe you can come and hang out with us sometimes. Maybe with your cousin."

Payden's smile turned on me. "I told you he was great, right?"

"Right."

Payden gave me another secret smile and turned back to Elsie. "I'm glad you're okay."

She nodded, and they stared at each other for a couple more long seconds, and then Payden had to go inside. "I'll talk to Mario about getting together."

"You do that."

We turned and retraced our steps to the car. "He's so nice," Elsie said. "He looks at me nicely. Not like—" She broke off.

"Like who?" I put the groceries in the back seat.

"Nobody," she mumbled. Her face was pale and her eyes glued to the ground.

I waited until we got in the car to say, "You can tell me

when you're ready. It won't surprise me. It isn't fair and it isn't right, but whatever happened, I promise you I'll do my best to see that it doesn't happen again."

Elsie lifted her eyes to mine. "I know. But some people . . . I just don't ever want to talk about him. It's like if I do, he'll find me."

"Okay," I said simply. At least she'd verified again that it was a "him" she'd been running from. Of all the girls I'd helped, so far the only woman who'd been abusive was Saffron's mother. Mothers were often neglectful, addicted, absent, or victims themselves, but not quite as prone to beating a child half to death.

When we arrived at the apartment, Makay was there with Nate. "Hey." She looked up at us from the couch where she cuddled her brother. Ruth and Halla were tickling his toes and trying to get him to come to them. Saffron was in the corner with her iPhone that she currently used only as an iPod, since she lost her cell phone service after her parents kicked her out.

Makay set Nate in Ruth's arms and came to help me put away the groceries. "Can I store a few packs of diapers here? I had some double coupons for them, but I don't dare leave them at Fern's. She has a great talent of turning baby items into cash for her drugs, and my roommates are almost as bad."

"Sure, come on."

Leaving Nate with the girls, Makay grabbed her grocery bag and followed me to the bedroom closet where I kept a large trunk with a heavy combination padlock. Though I mostly trusted the girls, it didn't make sense to tempt them, not with their background of survival.

So I kept the trunk, and each of them were allowed to put their private or personal belongings inside, separated into labeled flat rate boxes from the post office, which Makay had once pointed out was an improper use of the boxes and was probably prosecutable by law. One more thing for me to worry about. But the setup worked nicely, and nothing had been stolen or misplaced since I'd started it last January. None of us had much, so there was enough room for the two diaper packs.

"You don't have to put them in there," Makay said. "There's enough room on that top shelf."

"It's okay. I'd feel better being sure."

"So," Makay said, dropping onto one of the mattresses and bringing her knees to her chest. "I hear you have a new job."

"That's right. I'm really excited about it." I relocked the trunk and sat next to her on the mattress and told her about Teen Remake and the Back to Nature program. "It's different from what I'm doing now because the parents are involved, paying for the programs and working with their kids, but it'll be similar in a lot of ways, I'm guessing."

"You'll be great," Makay said. "Does this mean you don't have to go to your dad's sweat shop?"

I laughed. "Hardly. It just means maybe we can find a bigger place."

She shook her head. "Not with just one income. It's impossible."

"Maybe I can, if I'm an official foster parent."

Makay's eyes widened. "Seriously? That would be great! I mean, even a little bit that you can use for food and lodging would make a huge difference."

"I know, right?" I felt happy inside. Hopeful. "It means I'll be out late on Fridays, and Thursdays are going to be hard, since I'll have to go to both my jobs. At least on Thursdays I'll be working at Teen Remake instead of at the camp, so there isn't added driving time. But I was hoping you might stop by to check on Elsie for me. I don't like leaving her alone so long, and I'm not sure she's ready to run errands with the other girls."

"Sure, I'd be glad to." Makay rocked back on the mattress, her arms around her legs. At the moment she looked as young as Elsie, her dark hair almost as long.

"It won't interfere with your job?"

She frowned and shook her head. "Actually, I was fired from the restaurant. I went to drop off Nate yesterday morning because Fern had called me, bawling, late Wednesday night and said she wanted him. Usually when she does that, she's sober for a few days, and there's a neighbor there who keeps an ear out for Nate, just in case. But when I got there, she was passed out, and I had no one to watch him. I tried to call in sick, but apparently I've done that one too many times."

"You couldn't just bring him here?"

"I knew you would be taking the girls to their job."

"Saffron and Elsie were here."

She sighed. "Yeah, but I'd have still been late, and they gave me a boatload of warnings. It was be there on time or hit the road. Honestly, I can't blame them."

"What are you going to do about rent?" Before she answered, I hurried to add, "You know you're always welcome here."

"I have another gig coming up. It's only an occasional

job, but I've done it before in the past, and it usually gets me enough."

I didn't like the way her face blanched as she said it. "Doing what?"

"Basically, I'm a courier."

Something inside me screamed a warning. "It's not drugs, is it?"

"You kidding? After what drugs have done to Fern? No way. No drugs or alcohol involved. Basically, this guy tracks people down on the Internet and connects them with others who want to find them, mostly kids looking for their birth parents. I do some running around for him, delivering or picking up stuff. The only setback is that he's kind of a jerk. But I've known him for years, and he helped me survive after I left home as a kid." She frowned. "That was back when I thought I could find my birth parents."

"Wait, I thought your parents died."

"They were my adoptive parents."

How did I not know that? Poor Makay, losing her adoptive mother, then her father—though he hadn't been much of a prize to begin with—and now being stuck with her stepmother, Fern. "Well, like I said, you can always stay here."

"I know, but I hate to add to your burden. Seven women in a one bedroom, one bath apartment is too much already."

"They don't need much."

"I'll keep it in mind. Maybe we can find a bigger place together."

I stared at her. "Yeah, maybe so."

For a moment, my dream of a house seemed a step

closer. The foster parenting, Makay helping . . . but Makay had Nate to worry about, and her stepmother. She could barely afford the low rent she paid in the apartment she shared with five other girls, and having Nate with her so much made working even part time difficult. No, I needed to do it myself.

"What is it?" Makay asked, her dark eyes concerned.

"Ah, it's nothing. Thanks for agreeing to check in on Elsie. She's finally warming up a bit, and I don't want any setbacks."

"She'll be all right. Kids are resilient." If anyone knew that, it was Makay. I still didn't know how she'd survived on the street so young after her drunk father had married the horrible Fern.

Without warning, the partially ajar bedroom door slammed the rest of the way open. Ruth stood there, her eyes large. "Come quick, you got to see this! It's Halla—she's all over the Internet."

I leapt from the bed and followed her into the living room, where Saffron was booting up my computer. "Look!" she said, pushing her phone at me. I glanced at the picture on Saffron's Facebook page. It was Halla all right, though her hair was a few inches longer in the photo. No mistaking her blue eyes and the small, narrow nose. Instead of her customary army pants and tank top, she wore a pink T-shirt and her lips had been brushed with gloss. "Everyone is posting this," Saffron said. "She looks a little different, but it's obviously Halla. Anyone who sees this is going to know it's her."

I sat down in front of my laptop and put in the password. Sure enough, my own friends were posting the missing girl picture, which already had over five thousand shares. I glanced at Halla, who was standing by the couch, her eyes round and her face frightened.

"I won't go back," she said.

"Of course not." I thought a moment. "Look, we recognize her because we know her, but most people won't. Her hair is so short and with her camouflage, it's almost like a disguise."

"It'll pass," Makay predicted. "The next thing will come along and replace it. Everyone will forget in a few days."

Saffron shook her head. "There's more." She clicked on the link, and it went to a blog run by Halla's parents, who looked nice and normal and concerned. Smack dab in the middle of the page was a picture of Halla with her short hair and camouflage. "We believe she is now in Arizona," her father wrote. "We've left Idaho and will be staying in Arizona until we bring her home."

"He even has their pastor making a plea on a Go Fund Me account," Ruth said. "It's sick."

"How did they even get that picture?" Halla sank down on the couch beside me. "I didn't cut my hair until I left home."

Saffron's jaw clenched, her eyes blazing. "The jerk must have gotten it from someone at one of the homeless shelters you stopped at on the way here from Idaho."

"I'll have to leave," Halla whispered as I slipped my arm around her. "I'll have to run again."

Ruth squeezed in next to Halla and grabbed her hand. "I'll go with you. I ain't lettin' you go alone."

"No one's going anywhere," I told them. "We're all

sticking together. Makay's right—this will blow over. We just have to stay low until they move on. Meanwhile, I'll get certified as a foster parent, and talk to the lady I met yesterday and figure things out."

Elsie reached past Ruth and laid a small hand on Halla's shoulder. "I'll help Ruth with your jobs until they leave."

Halla's frozen face suddenly relaxed. "Thank you." She jumped up and hugged Elsie.

Saffron had turned my laptop toward her and was reading the rest. "Nothing here from your mother, Halla. Besides the picture of them together, it's only him. He says he's taken a leave of absence. They've raised a couple thousand dollars on the Go Fund Me, but it looks stalled now." She paused, considering. "I think we should give you a new look, make sure you always wear different clothes—"

"She could dress like a boy," Ruth said excitedly.

I looked at Halla doubtfully. "She wouldn't pass for a boy any more than you do in those clothes, but changing her appearance isn't a bad idea. And keeping her out of sight until this dies down. You willing to do that, Halla?"

She nodded. "If it means I don't have to leave. I've got a few books to read anyway."

"You can use my phone for a few weeks until I have enough for cell service," Saffron said. "I downloaded a ton of really great free books from mybookcave.com. They're even rated for content like movies." She hesitated before adding. "But I do have an idea. What if I post that this whole blog is a hoax?"

"Uh," I said, "maybe not. They can trace these things."

"There might be a way." Saffron smiled. "I met a new guy today. Computer whiz. I bet he'd know."

"You can't trust him!" Halla sounded panicked.

"Of course not. But that doesn't mean I can't learn a few things from him." There was a determination in Saffron's voice that I'd heard before. She was going to research this, whatever we said.

"You learn all you want," I told her. "But don't do anything until we talk."

She frowned but nodded slowly. "Okay."

Makay reached over and picked up Nate, who was clawing at her pant leg. "I might have some ideas on that myself," she said. "I know a guy who finds people, and I've learned a bit about how to make being found harder."

I snapped my fingers. "Now that's a great idea. You two work together. Saffron, just run everything past Makay, okay?" Since I had no time for social media and was barely on the Internet, Makay would police the situation better than I ever could. I believed in delegation.

"Halla," Makay said, "you haven't used your Facebook lately, have you?"

She shook her head. "Only twice since I left Idaho, and not since Lily brought me and Ruth home."

Home, meaning the old apartment. I still felt grateful my parents held their Thanksgiving celebration at noon, so I was able to drive back to find Ruth and Halla eating dinner at the church. If I hadn't found them, they wouldn't have discovered Zoey and Bianca a month later.

"That's good." To Makay, I added, "Let us know."

"Well, since we're staying in anyway," Saffron said, "who wants to do nails?"

"Me! Me!" yelled Nate.

We all laughed. They crowded around the small kitchen table, and as I listened to their chatter, I thought about how the girls had come into my life. Funny how the two largest family days of the year, Thanksgiving and Christmas, had each increased our little misfit family by two. Saffron had arrived first around Labor Day, and I'd found Elsie a few days after Easter, which had come in mid-April this year.

I couldn't help wondering who I might find on the Fourth of July.

Makay left to track down some coupon deals at the grocery store, and the girls spent the afternoon fiddling with Halla's appearance while I replaced the screws in my repaired cupboard door. After an hour, Saffron went out and bought a cheap brown wig, and that made all the difference.

I was touched that she'd spent the money she was saving for a car and phone service to help Halla. It was a far cry from when she and Zoey almost had fist fights over who was going to shower first, or when she accused Ruth of hoarding food.

I realized that somehow, at some point, they'd changed from a bunch of troubled, runaway girls into a family. A real family.

That only made me more determined to fight for them.

Ruth sat next to me on the couch, watching the final transformation. "I almost don't know you myself," she said to Halla. I had to agree. Halla still looked fourteen instead of sixteen, but with subtle makeup instead of thick black liner, dark hair, and normal clothes, she wasn't easily recognizable.

"Weird how hair can make such a difference." There was a wistfulness in Ruth's voice.

I turned to her. "We can do you next."

Her eyes dropped to her oversized pants. "I don't think so."

As if sensing her friend's distress, Halla stopped turning around and dropped to her knees in front of where we sat. "I told her she'd look beautiful in girl clothes, but she doesn't want to look beautiful."

"Well, she's beautiful anyway," Saffron said, hands on her hips as she stared down on us. "I bet you could be a model."

Ruth's face paled. "I hate being pretty. My mom says it's my fault her boyfriends couldn't help themselves."

I'd told her before that what happened to her wasn't her fault, but this was the first time she'd admitted that her mother also blamed her. "Well, your mother is plain wrong. It's their fault—and hers. You were only thirteen. She should have protected you." Her eyes lifted to mine, and I hoped I was getting through. "You have every right to be beautiful and dress beautifully and not be afraid of being attacked by scumbags pretending to be men. Real men don't attack women, and certainly not kids. I'm not saying you should go around half-naked or walk into dangerous situations—that would be stupid—but you have the right to be safe in your own home. And you are perfectly safe here."

There was no doubt in my mind that Ruth needed

counseling, but we didn't have access to that, not yet. All she had was me and the others. I'd researched myself crazy on this, and most of it boiled down to love, patience, security, and reassurance. I hoped it was enough.

"I know I'm safe now," Ruth said. "But if they send me back again—"

"Not going to happen," Halla retorted. "Come on. Let's dress you up."

Ruth was weakening. "Well, maybe it would be okay, just for a little while."

"Yes!" Saffron clapped her hands and went to dig in the closet. She couldn't find any pants long enough, but some tan shorts and a fitted white tee did wonders. I still hadn't figured out how to style Ruth's frizzy hair, but we braided it in tiny cornrows that made her eyes and face stand out. I'd really have to see if Bea from DCS could give me any hair pointers. Of course, that might mean telling her about Ruth. Maybe soon.

That was when Zoey and Bianca arrived home from school, having caught their usual ride with friends. Zoey's jaw dropped, and Bianca did a double take. "Wow," Zoey said. "You two look so different! For a moment, I thought Lily had brought home some new girls."

"Yeah, me too." Bianca fingered Halla's wig. "Can I try it on?"

"Yes! Ugh, it's getting hot anyway." Halla slipped it off.

"Who wants chocolate chip cookies?" I asked. The girls cheered and chatted together in the kitchen, snapping pictures with my phone until the cookies were ready.

Five o'clock had rolled around before I got up the nerve to text Jameson. So, I wrote, *what time are you off?*

Just left.

Want to see a movie?

A long pause and then he sent: *I have something better in mind. Is that okay?*

More than okay. At least he wasn't bailing on me. *Sure.*

Pick you up at six?

I could pick you up.

No, that's okay. I'd rather drive the Mustang, if you don't mind.

I'm fine with that.

I looked up from my phone to find Ruth staring at me. She appeared eighteen with her transformation, but no doubt in four years when she really was eighteen, she'd still look the same. "So, does he like the movie idea?"

"He says he has something better in mind."

Saffron squealed. "Ooh, I can't wait! We'd better do your makeup now."

I let the girls fuss over me and choose my clothing—a rather snug pair of jeans and a fitted Hard Rock Café T-shirt from Cabo San Lucas, where my parents had once taken Tessa and me on a cruise. I'd been collecting Hard Rock shirts for years, though all the European ones except London had been gifts from my mother's friends.

"I don't even know where we're going," I protested. "What if it's someplace nice?"

"If there was a dress code, he'd have told you," Saffron said.

I was beginning to have second thoughts. Surprises usually weren't good these days. "But I forgot tonight's our movie night."

"Not when you have a date," Zoey said. "Stop trying

to find excuses to stay home. Besides, we're moving it to Saturday, right?"

"And Halla can't go nowhere right now," Ruth added, "so we'll all hang here and watch TV without you. We're fine with that."

"Or we can grab some movies from Redbox," Bianca suggested.

"Remember, I have a date tonight too." Saffron gave me a mischievous grin. "But I won't be late if you won't."

"Deal." We shook on it, and then I took Zoey, Bianca, and Elsie to pick out some movies.

We passed our second-floor neighbor on the landing, and his eyes wandered over us, pausing briefly on Elsie, but the girl was in the middle of the others and didn't seem to notice. What was his obsession with her anyway? One thing was certain: the sooner I got out of this dump, the better.

By the time we returned with three DVDs, Jameson was already there. We found him pacing outside the apartment, his hiking boots loud on the concrete landing.

Hiking boots?

"Ah, there you are," he said, flashing the smile that made me feel as if I were the only person in the world. He must practice that smile in the mirror at home. "I was beginning to think you stood me up." That made the girls giggle.

"Nope," I said. "Remember, I was the one who asked you." I opened the door with my keys and ushered everyone inside.

Halla and Ruth stared at us from the couch, and I felt

a rush of pride that they hadn't cracked the door even to "hot" Jameson. Halla was wearing her wig again, and Ruth was still wearing my clothes.

"Hey," Jameson said to them. "You two look nice. Did you dress up for me? What's with the wig, Halla?"

"Aw, you're not supposed to recognize me." Halla stuck out her bottom lip in a pout.

"Well, I almost didn't. But there was no mistaking your sidekick. Honestly, Ruth, I'm loving those braid thingies in your hair. You're going to have to show me how you do those."

It was exactly the right response. No comment about her beauty or the clothes showing her figure—just that she looked nice, and he liked the cornrows.

"We thought you was gonna leave when we didn't answer the door," Ruth said. "We bet on it."

"No way. It's not every day I get asked out by a pretty girl."

"Where're you taking her?" This, surprisingly from Elsie.

"It's a secret," he whispered, winking at me, "but she'll tell you when we get back." Then he saw the DVD in her hands. "What, seriously? You found a Redbox with a copy of *Back to the Future?* No way. I always have to find that somewhere else. No one stocks classics these days."

I gaped. "You think that's a classic?"

"You bet! And if we didn't already have plans, we could stay right here and watch it."

That was going overboard. "Come on," I said. "We're out of here. Girls, you know where the leftovers are from last night. Enjoy dinner." To Jameson, I added, "I hope these plans include something to eat because if they don't, we—"

"They do," he said. "But you'll need a jacket."

I grabbed one from the small closet by the door. With a final glance at the girls, who were grinning at me and giving me the thumbs-up when Jameson wasn't looking, I closed the door behind me. I didn't remind them to lock the deadbolt, but I stayed close until I heard it.

Jameson grinned at me. "They'll be okay. We won't be long."

Strangely, I felt comforted.

Once again, Jameson drove us to South Mountain, but not to where we'd watched the sunrise. This place had a lodge, three cabins, and a small stage set before rows of stadium-like benches. Teens emerged from the lodge, talking and laughing.

Jameson grabbed my hand. "Come on. If we miss dinner, I don't know if I have enough strings to find us anything." He waved at some teens as they passed.

"Teen Nature?" I guessed.

"Yep. I thought it might be a good idea to get you acclimatized before you jump into the fire next week."

"It's really cool. I'm not sure what I expected—they told me there weren't tents—but this is more like a . . ."

"A motel in the mountains?" He laughed when I nodded. "I told you it wasn't a wilderness survival thing.

We do a lot of getting back to nature, but we don't want kids to hate it. We even have showers."

He opened the door at one edge of the lodge, and we walked into a cafeteria. There were two lines of food, but one had already shut down, and the workers looked ready to clean the other one up too. Jameson hurried over, grabbing both of us a tray.

"Hey, guys," he said to the two young men and the young woman, who were all near my age or maybe a year or two younger, "this is Lily. She starts next week. I thought I'd bring her to see what she's getting into."

"Hey," said the men together.

The woman smiled and waved. "Good to see another woman around here."

Jameson introduced them, but I only caught the woman's name—Dalia—before I was distracted by the food and my rumbling stomach. It was soft tortillas with all the fixings, and little containers with sherbet ice cream for dessert.

Jameson pointed to a group of kids still at a table. "We usually have about fifty kids up here each time, and twenty counselors. And some parents."

"The parents stay all night too?" I heaped a portion of taco meat onto my tortilla.

"Some do—not all of them. Not all the counselors stay, either. Only a certain number are required to, and only those few employees get paid for sleeping here. It's a great way to put in your forty hours." He grinned. "So I always opt for it when I can, now that I have enough seniority to be considered. I'll be sleeping here on Friday nights starting next week, and cutting down my day shifts accordingly."

I was glad they hadn't asked me to stay overnight, even though the drive out here to South Mountain on both Friday and Saturday would make my shifts longer. I might sleep better in a real bed here, but I'd worry too much about the girls.

We laughed and joked for the few minutes it took us to eat our food. The sun was already out of sight in the sky when we finished, though it was still fairly light, and Jameson took me to the benches in front of the stage, where the kids were gathering.

"You've got to see these skits," he said. "They've had only today to work on them. Some make you feel like you're back in kindergarten, but every now and then you get some really brilliant ones."

Numerous teens greeted Jameson as we approached, offering high-fives or complicated handshakes. They gave me subtle glances, but when Jameson introduced me, it wasn't as a future camp counselor, which made everyone assume I was his girlfriend. I decided I was okay with that for now.

There were six skits, and to my surprise, a few parents participated as well. The first four skits were funny only because they were so awful, but the fifth, a parody of a hospital stay, had me laughing out loud.

"That kid in the bed?" Jameson whispered. "His mother died last year, and that was when he started giving his father trouble. He's been writing some short stories, and I'm pretty sure this idea is based on one of those—very cathartic for him." The boy had brooding eyes, and he delivered every line with deadpan humor, but every now and then a smile escaped his control.

He's going to be okay, I thought.

The final skit was heads above most of the other presentations, but only half as good as the hospital one. "Okay, let's vote by clapping," said a counselor in a blue shirt with Teen Nature stamped in bold across his chest. The microphone squawked with feedback, and he grimaced before continuing.

The hospital skit won a standing ovation, and the actors received oversized chocolate bars and pats on the back for encouragement. "Okay, card games in the lodge," said the counselor, "but don't stay too late. Remember we have Chat Time in the morning, bright and early at six."

The kids booed, but only softly, and no one seemed very upset as they beelined for the lodge.

"Well?" Jameson asked, his arm around me as we sat close together on the bench. "How do you like it?"

"This is what I'll be helping with on Fridays?"

"In the evenings, at least. How are your acting skills?"

I thought of my roommates, school officials, and my mother. "Pretty good, I think."

"Then you have nothing to fear. Earlier, they had trust exercises, activities, and counseling sessions led by certified therapists. You'll get the hang of it, but I didn't want you to be in complete shock your first day on the job."

"It looks really great." I wanted to help the kids here, but I was even more excited about the things I'd learn to help my girls.

He offered a hand, and I took it, allowing him to pull me to my feet. "Come on. I'll show you my favorite spot."

He led me along a path and up some wooden stairs laid into the mountainside and then down another path, his footsteps sure in the dark. Obviously, he knew the place well. "There," he said, as we rounded a bend in the path that opened up to the valley below.

"Oh," I said, the word coming out as a partial sigh. "It's beautiful." In the distance, we could see city lights shining and twinkling like an early Christmas display. Even better were the overhead stars, glistening in an uninterrupted blanket of darkness, infused with mystery and magic.

"Stars are always brighter here than in the city." Jameson stood close, our jacketed arms touching.

"It's like a surprise, appearing around that bend so unexpectedly."

He chuckled. "Yeah, just like our so-called date."

I turned to face him. "You knew?"

"That you were referring to work? That you weren't really asking me on a date? Oh, yeah."

Now I understood the gleam in his eyes. It hadn't been excitement at being with me, but rather enjoyment at my slip. "Why didn't you say something?"

The moonlight illuminated his face, and there was no mistaking the way his eyes drank me in. "And miss out on my opportunity to do this . . ." Deliberately, he placed his lips on mine. Warmth flooded through me in a delicious, heady rush.

Okay then. I didn't know what to say, so I kissed him more deeply. He tasted of the mint gum we'd had after dinner, with maybe a hint of hot sauce, which turned out to be an intoxicating combination. His arms went around my back, anchoring me in the moment. He was significantly taller than I was, but our bodies fit together effortlessly.

Slow down, I told myself.

I didn't listen.

He pulled me closer, his hands running over my back on top of my jacket. My stomach fluttered, my heart pounded, and my mind was full of nothing but him. Being here like this, having him hold me—it was new and familiar all at once. A contentment I'd never experienced settled over me.

After long moments, Jameson drew reluctantly away. "I guess we should get going," he said, his breath short and his voice husky.

"Yeah." I had no idea what time it was. It could have been three days for all the awareness I had of anything besides him.

"If we hurry," he added, reaching for my hand, "we might be able to catch the last of *Back to the Future.*"

"Oh, brother." I rolled my eyes, but I was glad. Halla had been upset about her father's disruptive activities on the Internet, and I wanted to see if she was still as okay with everything as she'd been after the makeover. Because I wasn't as sure as I'd acted that I could keep her safely hidden.

I was still thinking of Halla and what to do about her all the way to the car, down the mountainside, and most of the drive back to Phoenix. As if sensing my preoccupation, Jameson kept up the conversation, talking about the camp and the kids, but I was only half listening.

"What are you thinking?" Jameson asked, sending me a worried glance. "Is it all more than you bargained for?"

"Oh, no. Sorry. It's just something that happened today with Halla."

"Something, by chance, that explains the wig?"

Internally, I cursed his perceptiveness. "Maybe." I wanted to tell him, to share the burden, but months of keeping certain things to myself stilled my tongue.

His hand slipped across the space between us, landing on my thigh and sending spikes of electricity through my nerves. "You can tell me. I mean, if you want."

I made the decision the way I always had with the girls—with my heart. It hadn't led me astray yet. "Remember how I told you that Halla escaped from a room her father had locked her in?"

"For six months, right? Until she jumped out the window and broke her arm."

I nodded. "Well, he's somehow tracked her here. There are pictures of her plastered all over Facebook and elsewhere on the Internet. He's saying he won't leave Arizona until he finds her. We saw the pictures today, and it freaked Halla—all of us—out."

"Sounds like he really wants to find her."

"It's more than that. I'm afraid she'll run again. Because if he knew where she was, he'd come for her, and I . . ." Would he think I was exaggerating? "I don't know if she'd survive it."

"You need to talk to Bea about her."

"What? No! It's only Halla's word against his. Her mother knows, but apparently she's a spineless idiot. Remember, Halla already gave in to despair once when she jumped out that window. I can't let that happen again."

Jameson didn't say anything but stared at the road

ahead. I wished he'd say something—anything. His hand was still on my leg, but I wanted it off. I wished I hadn't sat in the middle seat.

"Did you ever consider that maybe Halla is stretching the truth?" he said finally.

"No." I was offended that he'd even suggest it. I was glad when he reached an intersection and he had to lift his hand to shift. Maybe it was my silence or my stiffness, but he didn't return his hand to my leg. I felt both glad and bereft, which made no sense.

"Kids do that all the time. You know that—you have to know that."

Anger flooded me, as hot as the passion I'd felt for him earlier. "He *starved* her and locked her in a room. She tried to kill herself because her life was so bleak."

"That's what she says. Did you see her arm broken?"

"No, it had healed by the time I found her. She went to a free clinic and had the cast cut off on her way here from Idaho."

Jameson glanced over. "There are two sides to every story, and I've seen a lot of kids and parents at Teen Remake butt heads because neither side is willing to bend."

"Are you saying Halla's a liar? Because I'm telling you she's not. I've known her for six months. You've known her for, what, three days?" Questioning her was the same as questioning my judgment, because I'd taken her in.

"It doesn't take much for these kids to begin to believe what they're saying. Perceptions vary, and time changes perceptions. Besides, if her father does want her back, maybe he's willing to make changes. Being with a parent is the best thing for a child, if they're willing to make changes for the better."

"Not if he abuses her. Look, I don't want to talk about this anymore. Just take me home."

We were already on the street heading to the apartment. When he pulled into our lot, Jameson said, "I'm only saying you need to check out both sides. That's where Bea comes in. Just like you, I want Halla to be safe and happy. What if Halla is exaggerating and she belongs with her parents? I've seen it happen so many times at Teen—"

"At Teen Remake!" I finished. "You said yourself they never have the toughest cases. You have parents paying for their children to go to camps and for themselves to get training. Those parents want the best for their kids. Generally they're not hurting them, right?"

"That's true, but—"

I pushed opened the door. "You only know a tiny slice of what these girls have been through. You're not the one who was with Halla six months ago when her body was so wasted she could do little more than sleep. Halla's not a liar. But now you want to tell everyone about her—and you probably will, just like you did with Zoey and Bianca."

"What are you saying? How do Zoey and Bianca figure in this conversation?"

"*I* should have been the one who decided to tell Bea about them after I checked her out."

"But I thought—"

"You thought wrong. It was *my* choice! I'm the one who cares for them, not you. I'm the one who's sacrificing to feed them. I'm the one who comforts them when they cry with their nightmares."

"I'm not saying we turn Halla over. I just think we ought to research—"

I hopped out of the car, my voice rising with my anger. "You go ahead and do all the research you want. The fact remains that if you report this, it'll boil down to what it always has—Halla's word against her father's. Before she ran away, she went to school counselors. She even went to her pastor, and the only thing that happened was that they told her father, and he locked her up. And you know what? I can't trust someone who doesn't believe me. It's as simple as that. I think it's better for all of us if you don't come here anymore." I slammed the door hard.

For a moment, I felt a sharp satisfaction at the sound of the door and the hurt on his face. But every step away from him felt like an ever-widening chasm we could never cross. Why did he have to be so stubborn? Why did he have to interfere?

Because if I had to choose between them, there was really no choice. I was all Halla and the other girls had. Not that Jameson would care. He probably had women lined up to take my place—if I'd even meant anything real to him in such a short time.

I sprinted up the stairs, almost running into my second-floor neighbor, who let out something that might have been a chuckle or maybe a cough. I didn't wait around to decide which. On the fourth floor landing, I glanced out to see Jameson standing by his car, looking up at me. His earnest expression reminded me of our kisses on the mountain.

I shouldn't have told you, I thought. I didn't even tell my sister most of what happened to the girls, and she was on my side. My heart was usually right, but this time, I'd endangered Halla—and all the girls.

"Lily!" Elsie exclaimed as I walked into the apartment. The others crowded around me, asking questions: "Where's Mario?" "How'd the date go?" "Did he kiss you again?"

I held up a hand. "Okay, guys, I know you like Jameson, but I'm not sure I like him enough, you know? Just because he's hot, doesn't mean I'm going to fall in love with him or something."

"Oh, beans!" Ruth said.

Zoey shrugged. "Love's overrated anyway."

To distract them from more questions, I hurried to say, "Did you watch all of the videos?"

"We still have *Back to the Future* left," Ruth said. "We saved it in case . . . never mind."

Great. Just great. I grabbed the video from the stack on the television. "Put some more popcorn in, Halla," I said. "Let's get this show on the road."

The girls fell asleep long before the movie ended, and Saffron came home before one, as she promised. Double-checking the locks, I left the girls sleeping together like a bunch of newborn kittens and climbed up on the roof, where I sat looking at a muted version of the stars Jameson and I had seen from the mountain. A single tear rolled down my cheek as I thought about the blanket of magic. I wiped it away.

I had to make sure Jameson didn't interfere further. I'd have to keep him away. I'd lie outright, if necessary.

If I didn't let him into my life, he couldn't do something I'd forever regret.

A small hand slipped into mine, startling me. "Oh, hi," I murmured to Elsie, who snuggled her head against my shoulder.

"You're sad," she said.

"A little."

"Because of him?"

"Yeah."

"Men suck."

Her serious tone made me smile, until I realized she wasn't kidding. "Not Payden," I said. "Not every man."

She sighed. "Well, Payden's not really a man yet, is he?"

She had a point. We sat there for a few minutes, staring at the muted sky.

"Lily?"

"Yeah?"

"I wish you were my mother."

Her mother. Should I ask what she was like? No, not tonight. It was too soon—at least according to my gut, which, given the fiasco with Jameson, might not be working anymore.

I pulled her tighter. "I wish that too."

On Monday evening, I left Teen Remake feeling depressed after a foster parent class on the effects of abuse and neglect on children. The concepts weren't new to me. Zoey had cut her arm again over the weekend to relieve stress after her chat with Bea at school on Friday, Bianca had issues talking to adults, Halla would barely eat, and Ruth still dressed like a boy. Saffron's flippancy about her dates worried me as well.

So I'd seen firsthand the effects of child abuse, but it wasn't anywhere near as severe as the stories I'd heard in class tonight. Some of those were horrific and left a distaste in my mouth and the urge to climb a tall building and scream my lungs out at the injustice.

Thankfully, my girls were comparatively well adjusted—and I was honest enough to admit it was probably due more to their own resilience and mutual support than to my nurturing.

I'd sat through another class about loss and grief the Saturday before, the day after my disastrous date with Jameson, and I'd viewed two presentations online about discipline and sexual abuse. The discipline problems had surprised me because the girls and I had been too busy surviving to worry about making or breaking many rules. I enforced only the bare essentials, instinctively doing the right thing about curfews and dealing with stealing.

The sexual abuse class had shown me nothing new, but it was a sober reminder. Since Ruth came to live with me, and then Zoey, I'd researched the topic so much that I felt I could teach a class on it myself. Still, after I'd watched the video on Sunday, I'd had the urge to wash my entire body and scrub out my eyeballs, and maybe go to church and confess to a priest for having even taken the class. It was unspeakably terrible what children endured at the hands of those who were supposed to protect them.

At least I'd made significant headway on the thirty hours I needed to finish my foster parent training, and that was my current goal: get that finished so I could become official.

I hadn't expected to see Jameson at either of the two classes held at Teen Remake, but I looked for him anyway, wishing things had gone differently between us. Was there any possibility he could be right about Halla? On Friday I'd been certain she hadn't lied to me, but the class tonight had shown me that desperate children were capable of far worse than lying if that meant protecting themselves from further pain. But if she wasn't in pain to begin with, if she'd lied about it, what would she be lying for?

I had to stop this. If I couldn't trust my own judgment, how could I help the girls?

"Lily, wait!"

I turned to see Bea Lundberg coming from the building.

She had introduced the speakers tonight, so I'd seen her here, but now I tensed, wondering if Jameson had told her about Halla. "Hi, Bea."

"I just wanted to let you know that I've been busy this weekend." She flashed me a smile. "Zoey and Bianca's uncle is everything you said he is. I definitely know his kind."

Hope spilled through the barrier I'd made around my heart. "He signed them over?"

"He could hardly sign fast enough when he realized that if he didn't, there would be an inquiry, and he'd have to pay child support. I had the papers completed at my DCS office today with our attorney, and I have a temporary foster care assignment for you that will be in place until after our home visit and your training completion. We'll need you to sign a few things."

"That's great. Thank you so much!"

"Will tomorrow morning be a good time to visit?"

"Yeah. The girls won't be home, though, if that's important. And I work in the afternoon."

"That's okay. The caseworker assigned to you will have to meet the girls at some point, but my talk with them is enough for now. You will be receiving a stipend for both girls, but checks are always post-paid for each month. So the money will start accruing today, and you'll get a check around the first of July for these last few days of May and all of June."

At an average of twenty dollars a day, I'd be able to make the rent for July and pay for food without dipping into my savings or asking Tessa for help. I could actually buy Zoey that new pair of jeans she desperately needed, and get Bianca an appointment for an eye exam. Maybe someday we could buy a bedframe. "Thank you," I said, barely able to speak past the lump of emotion that had somehow lodged itself in my throat.

Bea smiled. "I'm glad to help. Now why don't you verify your address for me? Unless you're still at the same place that's on the court documents."

I shook my head. "No, we moved."

"Glad I asked. Caseworkers hate it when I send them to the wrong place."

"Okay." I wrote it down for her, realizing that meant they could show up anytime now. I needed to make sure the girls knew, and that we had a plan to hide the truth about how many lived there. Zoey and Bianca shared the double mattress, which wasn't approved, and having four girls in such a tiny room was never permitted. We'd have to do some juggling, and keep all but one of our fold-out mattress chairs folded when we weren't using them. Maybe I'd even move Elsie's to the living room. She seemed to be falling asleep on my couch more often than not these days anyway.

Tomorrow Ruth and Halla were supposed to be doing errands for their ladies, but we hadn't decided what we were going to do about Halla yet. The disguise would probably be enough, unless one of their clients had seen the Facebook posts.

Bea turned to leave, but I stopped her. "Hey Bea, this might be a weird question, but how do you get your hair to look like that? I know this girl, and she's been trying to get her hair to look . . . well, anything other than a frizzy mess. Braids only go so far."

"Oh, I hear you there. Let me tell you, the first few times aren't easy, but if you have the right products, it's not too difficult to keep up once you figure it out." She launched into a long explanation, which had me jotting notes on my phone. I wished I could just bring Ruth to her, but I had to talk to Ruth's mother first. I wasn't sending her back to be abused.

Maybe it was Bea's success with Zoey and Bianca's uncle, or her easy sharing of her hair tips, but instead of going home, I drove the twenty minutes to Glendale where Ruth's mother lived in a tiny run-down house in a neighborhood that looked sapped of life. The front light was on, and one inside as well, so I went up the walk, my can of pepper spray in my jacket pocket, and knocked on the door.

No one answered. I was about to leave when a crash inside alerted me to someone coming. I turned back around as a woman opened the door. Her black hair was cut to less than an inch, and her brown eyes dominated her small, narrow face. Ruth's eyes, but that was all Ruth had gotten from this woman. Ruth's mother was two shades lighter and at least a foot shorter, and while she was pretty, she had none of Ruth's beauty. The bags under her eyes and the small bruises on her upper arm, in the shape of a man's hand, screamed abuse of some sort.

"Can I help you?" she asked, her lip quirking a bit and showing a dark spot on her right canine tooth, near the gum.

"I'm sorry to bother you this late," I said. "Are you Wanda? I'm a friend of Ruth's."

"Ruthie?" Her eyes narrowed. "She ain't in trouble, is she? Because I ain't responsible. She's fourteen and does what she wants."

"No, nothing like that . . . it's just"—I took a deep breath before plunging on—"I'd like to talk to you about getting her into school. She's really bright, and I've been working with her this past year. I think she could get in and catch up without too much trouble, but she's going into high school, and after that, it's a lot harder. Do you have a moment to talk about it?"

"Yeah. You come on in."

She opened the door wider, and I entered a room that was almost as small as our living room. Stacks of clothes cluttered the stained carpet, and she gathered up several used plates and cups so I could sit on the couch, which looked like real leather and was nice compared to the rest of the room. Or maybe it only seemed so in the dim light.

"So how could you help her?" Wanda asked, sitting next to me.

I tried not to stare at a dark, unidentifiable smear on the wall. "I'd like to become a foster parent to Ruth." No use sugarcoating it. "That way I can get her clothing and medical care."

Wanda had gone stiff the moment I mentioned foster care. "Is this about what happened last year? I told the social worker I don't know what went on. I wasn't home. But she throws herself at my boyfriends, just like I said. It ain't really their fault."

"What?" The idea of shy Ruth throwing herself at a man was absurd. Was that why the caseworker had sent her back?

"I told her she could come or go as she wants," Wanda added. "I'm fine with that, but I heard they make you pay for foster care."

"I don't think so, not if you can't afford it."

"Yeah, they'll make me pay, or take her away."

"Well, would it be so bad if they were responsible for her? She only has a few years left in school."

Wanda's hand went to her chest. "Give up my baby? What kind of mother do you think I am? I don't want to give her up. I need my baby. And she don't have to worry. I have a new boyfriend now, not that white trash I was with before." Her eyes fell from mine to scan the messy room. "I'm sure he'll be fine with her here, especially if she helps clean up."

The sinking feeling in my chest grew. Clearly, Wanda wasn't willing to sign Ruth over to the state, allow foster care, or admit there was a problem. "What if Ruth doesn't want to come home? Would you consider a temporary guardianship situation—just for school?"

She snorted. "She's a child. She's got to do what I say, and I want her home. I've been meaning to track her down, soon as I had the time. When she gets back here, she can go to school."

Her daughter had been gone for over six months and only now she wanted to find her? Wanda was a study in contradiction: one minute she was saying Ruth did her own thing, and in the very next breath, Ruth was a child who should obey her mother.

"Is he home? Your boyfriend, I mean." I didn't really want to meet him, but foster parent training had drilled into me the importance of reuniting families when possible. Maybe this new man was good for Wanda and Ruth. Maybe Wanda was sincere in wanting her daughter.

She shoved off the couch, leaning heavily on her arm to do so. "Sure. I'll go get him. Then you can tell Ruth to come on home."

She returned with a short, wiry black man, with a bald head and a trim beard. "She's here about Ruth," she said by way of introduction.

He laughed and reached out a hand, which I let him take. "I can't wait to meet Ruth." He winked at me, and for an instant, I could see the charm that might have attracted Wanda. "From the pictures I see she's a beauty, just like her momma. I'm fine with her coming back, if that's what you're here to ask—you're one of them social workers, right?" He stood with his hands inside his pockets, jingling some keys or change. "Course she'll have to help out 'round here. We get food stamps for her, but everyone has to pull their weight."

"Food stamps," I repeated. At least that tidbit of information shed more light on Wanda's unwillingness to let Ruth go to a foster home.

"Baby, she don't need to hear about that," Wanda cooed, wrapping an arm around his waist and staring at him pointedly.

He leaned over to kiss her lips. "I just meant that I got me some ideas on how Ruth can help out. She's a fine-looking girl, and I got a friend that has a bar—not that she'd serve alcohol, of course—but there's always dishes to wash." He didn't meet my eyes as he spoke; in fact, they wandered everywhere but to my face.

He's lying, I thought. But about what part? "A bar, huh? Sounds interesting. What's your name, by the way?"

A fleeting discomfort marred his face. "Tyron Fisher."

I took out my phone and wrote it down. "Okay, we'll be in touch."

"Wait!" Wanda's fingers dug into my shoulder as I headed for the door. "I'm still getting the food stamps for her, right? You ain't taking them away?"

Tears for Ruth stung my eyes. "I'm just here to see if I can get Ruth enrolled in school. I don't have anything to do with food stamps."

"Oh. All right. Then tell her we're waiting for her. She'll have to sleep on the couch, though. We got borders staying in her old room."

"Couple of my friends," Tyrone added.

Great. The guy with the bar, no doubt.

I hurried back to my car, reaching it before the tears fell. Not one question about how Ruth was doing, or if she was happy. I wasn't sending her back here. No, I had all summer to figure out what to do before Ruth was supposed to start high school, but I wasn't giving her back to this woman and her creepy boyfriend.

I drove down the street with my lights off for a good block, in case they snuck out of the house to write down my license plates. If they actually went searching for Ruth, they wouldn't be able to connect her to me.

Back at the apartment, I checked my face in the car mirror, to make sure there was no trace of tears. I wasn't falling apart—or at least not where the girls could see. There had to be a way. Bea had gone to battle for me with Zoey and Bianca's uncle. Could she do the same for Ruth? I clung to the hope that she would, or that I could find a larger place and have more official foster children to help pay for Ruth's needs.

A knock on my window startled me, and my head jerked toward it, expecting the girls, or even my second-floor neighbor, which had me wishing I'd locked the door. Instead, it was Jameson. Warmth rushed through me at the sight of him, followed by an equal amount of coldness, all of which I was sure was reflected in my face.

"Can I come in?" he said, his voice muffled. "I need to talk to you."

I nodded and waited as he slipped inside the car, shutting the door after him. "Don't you know how to text?"

"Don't you know how to answer them?" A hint of a smile softened his response.

Admittedly, I hadn't looked at my phone since using it to find Wanda's house. "I've been occupied."

"I guessed that." He gestured to my face. "What happened?"

"You mean why am I upset? Oh, I don't know. Besides parents hurting their children and my having no way to protect them, and certain people thinking I'm the one keeping them from a happy family reunion, nothing."

He winced at the hardness in my tone. "Okay, I deserved that."

Something in me wilted at the admission. I didn't want to fight; I just wanted to sleep for a month straight. "Look, it's been a long day, and tomorrow I have to get ready for a visit from DCS, or whatever that department with fancy initials is called."

"I heard about Zoey and Bianca. That's great. It usually

takes three months to get approved, so I'm glad Bea was able to pull some strings to get the wheels going faster."

"It helped that the girls were already with me." I shut the mirror, feeling too exposed to him under its light.

"Look, you were right about Halla."

His words froze my hand on its way to the door handle. I turned back to him slowly and waited for more.

"I made a few calls to some friends I have in Idaho, and they made calls to their friends and so forth. I talked to a lot of people—no one official, but it raised enough flags to make me think Halla's father is exactly what she claims." He paused and ran a hand through his hair in a way that made my heartbeat pick up. There was a tiny scar on his chin that I'd never noticed before, and I wondered where he'd gotten it. "The neighbor actually told me if I knew where Halla was, I should hide her. She said Halla's mother used to be a friend of hers but when she started commenting about Halla's dad's strictness, the mother stopped calling."

"So you're not going to turn her in?"

"Is that what you think of me?"

"It sure seemed like it Friday night."

He sighed and leaned back. "I'm sorry. I really am. I just . . . Lily, you have to see that you can't do this alone. Are you going to finish school? What about the future? You know the girls need counseling and to go to school and live in a place that doesn't have questionable men lurking around."

"I'm changing all that. I'll get legit, find a big house, and put as many girls as I can there, even those I can't become an official foster parent for. I don't want . . .

I can't . . ." I couldn't finish. I didn't want to admit that I knew by experience how devastating it was to grow up feeling unloved—and I'd had it nowhere near as rough as my girls. I'd had Tessa and that had saved me, had allowed me to develop into a person who could love and care for others. My girls had no one except me and each other; I hoped that would save them.

He shook his head, but he was smiling. "When you say it, I believe you. There's this . . . light in your face, and I believe you completely."

"You do?"

"And I want to help."

I didn't know what that meant exactly, but I recognized the look in his eyes. Whatever else he meant, he also wanted to kiss me, and there was no way that was happening, not yet. Not until I could really trust him.

"Truce?" he said.

"Okay. But you do nothing about the girls unless I say. That means you don't talk to anyone about them being with me."

He tucked my hair behind my ear and ran his finger along my cheek, sending hot, exhilarating tingles to my stomach. "Deal. But you have to tell me why you were crying."

I couldn't, not after what had happened with Halla. What if he thought Ruth's mother wanted her back for the right reasons? No, for now, I wasn't going to trust him with anything more.

"I went to one of the foster-parent classes tonight. You know, trying to get my license. It's pretty horrible what children go through."

"I know. It's why I keep working at Teen Remake. I feel I'm making at least some difference. Anyway, I documented everything I learned about Halla's family, and we can use it if we need to. At sixteen, Halla will probably have a lot to say about what happens to her, especially if we can prove abuse."

"I can't risk it yet. She'll run—I know she will, and I'm not going to betray her. We need more solid evidence. So you'd better tell me right now if you plan to turn her in."

He shook his head. "We'll find another way."

The pressure building in my head eased. "I'd better go in," I said. "I'm already late. The girls will be wondering where I am." Besides, I didn't trust myself—a few kisses, and I'd probably be telling him everything again. Better to keep my distance completely.

"I'll walk you up."

I knew better than to object.

We hadn't yet reached the stairs when movement in a nearby car halted my progress. "Wait a minute. Is that . . .?" I hurried over to the car and tapped on the window. Sure enough, Saffron was inside, making out with her newest boyfriend. She jumped away from him and shot out the door, her hair looking almost as orange as Tessa's under the fluorescent street lighting.

"Saffron," I began.

She flashed me a grin as she slammed the door. "Don't worry. I already made that mistake once, and I'm never going to let a boy get that close again. You should know that by now. It was just a bit of harmless making out." She waved to the boy as he pulled away.

"Harmless?" Jameson said. "You know boys don't feel the same way about it, right?"

"Oh? You speaking from experience?" Saffron said. "I heard you two gave the girls a show the other night."

Jameson looked sheepish, and I felt my face flush. Hopefully, neither of them could see it in the darkness of the parking lot.

"That's different," I said. "I'm a lot older. I'm supposed to be . . ." What, trying to find a husband? So not going to say that in front of Jameson. It wasn't as if I was an old maid.

Saffron laughed. "I know. But I promise, I learned my lesson when I got pregnant. That's never going to happen again. Ever. I know there aren't many guys out there that are worth anything."

"Hey," Jameson protested.

"Okay, maybe you. But I hear the jury's still out on that one." With a flip of her hair, Saffron turned toward the stairs.

"Yeah I know." Jameson looked at me as we followed more slowly.

He was so appealing that I wanted to wrap my arms around him and kiss him senseless, but things were too up in the air between us right now. I thought he was on my side, but there was too much regulation in him. How could it possibly work between us?

After saying hello to the girls, Jameson left me at the door with a glance at Saffron and a chaste "friend" kiss on my cheek. Even so, his touch sent my heart racing again. Well, I'd given up a lot for the girls, and I could give him up too.

The minute the door was shut, the girls clustered around me. "I thought you weren't going to date him," Bianca said.

"Well, a woman can change her mind," Elsie put in.

"That's right, we can change our minds," I said. "But for now he and I are just friends."

Saffron rolled her eyes. "Sure, you are. Anyone can tell he is so into you. Like he said, it's not the same for guys."

"That doesn't mean I have to be into him." Time to change the subject. "Now why aren't you guys ready for bed? We have to be up bright and early."

"Why?" groaned Zoey, one of her long sleeves riding up enough to show that recent cut on her arm. "School is already early enough."

"Because DCS is coming to see this place, and we have to clean it and make it look like only you and Bianca live here." Bea knew about Saffron, but I wasn't sure how that might figure into the equation. If it came up, I could always say Saffron slept in the living room.

"Really? We're approved?" Zoey had started to sit on the couch, and now she jumped back up, her eyes wide.

"Well, temporarily, but yes." I hugged her and Bianca, and then Halla and Ruth, who were jumping up and down. "Someday you'll all be legit."

More jumping up and down and excitement until a pounding came on the floor from the apartment below. "Oops," I said. "Quiet down! Everyone to bed. Don't forget to brush your teeth. I can't afford a dentist."

As the girls scattered, Elsie's hand slipped into mine,

as if she were a much younger child. "It won't happen for me," she said. "My father will never let me go. He'd kill me first."

A chill crawled over my shoulders. The words that came to me were the ones Jameson had just said to me in the car: "Then we'll find another way."

E lsie went with Ruth on Tuesday to take care of the errands, while Halla walked over to Makay's. The apartment was all ready for DCS when the caseworker arrived. She was a plump, older woman with thin, bowl-cut hair, who seemed distracted and uninterested, breezing through the place without really seeing it. The only thing she wanted to verify was if the girls slept in the bedroom by themselves.

Calling on my high school drama classes, I smiled and pointed to Halla's chair bed next to the couch that we'd left unfolded. "I sleep in here, which works out well because I stay up later than the girls. I'm a student most of the time. Still got a couple years left. But we're hoping to get a two-bedroom apartment soon."

She nodded. "I'll be talking to the girls, of course, but this is as good as many foster homes I see. It's a good thing you're doing for them. Siblings this old are extremely hard to place together, especially where there's been sexual abuse. Do you have a boyfriend?"

"No. I don't usually even date." But unless that seemed

too weird, I hurried to say, "I have recently gone out a few times with a guy who works at Teen Remake."

"He doesn't sleep here, though?"

"Oh, no!"

She cracked her first smile at my shock. "Well, you'd be surprised what goes on. I don't like to place young girls in homes where boyfriends sleep over."

I thought of Ruth and had a surge of hope. "What if they're with their own mother?"

The social worker's face sobered. "That's the one exception. Unless the boyfriend has a record of some sort or is abusing the girls, we don't have much control over who the mother is sleeping with."

She took a final look around. "Do you have your landlord's approval letter?"

"I need his approval?" Uneasiness fluttered in my stomach.

She drew out a form from her binder. "Yeah. Just have him fill this out. It tells us he knows you're fostering the girls here and that it's all right."

"Okay." That shouldn't be too bad, admitting that two of the girls lived with me.

"Just send it in when you have it, or give it to Bea."

"I will."

"We'll schedule regular visits, but we'll let you know when. As long as everything works out with the girls, I think we're good for now."

"Thanks."

Just that fast, my dump of an apartment became Zoey and Bianca's official home.

When I arrived for my one o'clock shift at the factory, the receptionist told me my father wanted to see me in his office. Unease shifted through my mind, followed by a not-so-subtle increase in my heart rate. Until I'd begun working for him, Nolan Crawford had really been a non-entity to me. When we were young, Tessa and I had been careful to answer his questions promptly and not to upset him with our noise, but as he was home so rarely, it wasn't much of an issue. He was practically a stranger. I didn't know what his favorite color was, he'd never come to any of my plays, and aside from Christmas and the Fourth of July, we didn't act like a typical family. The factory in Phoenix was two hours away from our house in Flagstaff, and he'd more often than not stayed at his apartment in town, coming home on Thursday or Friday for the weekend. On the weeks he didn't return to Flagstaff, my mother wouldn't leave her bed. I didn't understand that until I was older and overheard him on the phone with a woman, whispering seductive things I'd never even imagined him saying to my mother.

When I entered his office, he looked over the reading glasses perched on his nose and gave me a smile that didn't reach his eyes. "Have a seat," he said, indicating a chair at the desk. His blond hair had streaks of gray, and he was carrying at least fifty extra pounds, but he exuded power.

I sat. You didn't say no to my father.

He watched me settle before dropping his gaze back to the report on his desk. "I heard your mother came to visit you at your new apartment?"

"Yes." This didn't sound good.

Again he looked up from his reading, his bushy eyebrows slightly drawn. "She's worried about you. She wants you to come home."

"I'm fine. Doing great, in fact. I love Phoenix."

"You can return here in the fall when you go back to college. Have you made the new changes to your schedule? I think you'll pick up French quickly enough." He looked down, as if the conversation had been concluded, though I knew he expected an answer.

"No, I haven't. Look, Dad, can we talk about this later? I'm going to be late for my shift."

His eyes met mine. "You no longer have a shift. That's what I'm trying to say. So you're free to go home and spend some time with your mother." He raised a hand before I could protest. "Your job will be waiting for you when you return to school in the fall." With that, he went back to his report.

Spend time with my mother? Was he joking? After she'd made me lose the job I needed to support the girls, knowing full well how devastating that would be for them and for me?

"I can't leave."

My father didn't look up for a full two seconds; then he leaned back and removed his glasses, keeping them in his hands. "Why not?"

"I'm doing some work at Teen Remake—helping kids.

I'm becoming licensed." I didn't mention licensed at what. "Please, I need this job."

"Does this have to do with those girls you have living with you? Lily, it's good you want to help, but you *will* go home and forget this nonsense. Your family needs you."

My family. I knew by the set of his jaw there was no use arguing. My father was always, always right, except when he wasn't, and then we all still pretended he was.

I stood slowly and started toward the door, pausing there. "You're right, they do need me. That's why I'm staying."

Shock registered on his face before he rose, as if his height would force me into compliance. "Lily—"

"Thank you for the offer of a job this fall, but I need a job now. I'll have to find something else."

"What about your schooling?" If his voice could be any more rigid, it might shatter with his next breath. "Does this mean you don't want help from us?"

It was a threat, but the only help they'd given me was this job, and if they used it as a way to control my life, how could I accept? "Actually, I could really use your help now by letting me keep my job."

"That's not possible."

"Right." I left before he could say any more, hurrying to my car, where I stared out the windshield, seeing nothing and feeling only shock.

What was I going to do? No more income from this job. That meant no better apartment. I had enough coming for June's rent, and whatever Teen Remake gave me in the meantime would have to do for food, but they barely paid above minimum wage, so that meant scraping by yet another month until the foster care check arrived in July. Even with that, I wouldn't be able to save enough for a down payment and first month's rent on another place.

Wiping away the tears, I drove to Tessa's apartment. I needed my big sister. She took one look at my face and hurried me over to her couch. "What happened?"

"Dad fired me because Mom wants me home. I told him no."

Tessa's freckled face flushed with her shock. Only she understood what it was to stand up to him. Slowly, a smile spread across her face. "Good for you! I'm proud of you."

"Really? I'm not being stupid?"

She hugged me. "No. You're my hero. And you're a hero to those girls."

"What if I can't pay the rent? Or buy food?"

"I'll help you. And you can get another job." Tessa drew away and looked into my eyes. "Besides, you hate it there. I know you do. We should be celebrating."

A bit dazed, I sat there as her comments sank inside me, pushing past the paralyzing fear. Deeper and deeper until they reached my heart. My sister was right, and now that she mentioned it, the idea of never going back to the factory made me feel giddy with happiness.

"I'm free," I whispered. "Free!"

"Now that's what I'm talking about." Tessa gave me a high five. "The factory's not right for you, and if Dad and Mom had any idea of who you are, they'd know that.

I know what you want: your dream house, helping the girls."

"But what about you?" I thought she hated working there just as much.

Tessa shrugged. "It's different for me. I don't mind the factory for now. I like the people I work with."

"Yeah. I did too." My co-workers were the only thing that had made it tolerable.

"Speaking of which, I think I'd better jump in the shower and get ready for work." Tessa rose from the couch. "I'll talk to Mom and Dad," she added. "Let's just give them a few weeks to settle down."

"Maybe by the Fourth." That was still over a month away.

She laughed. "Maybe."

When I arrived at my apartment, I found Makay mixing up the ingredients from my chocolate chip cookie recipe, while Halla played cars with Nate. Halla wasn't wearing her wig as she had been when she'd gone to Makay's that morning.

"Home already?" Makay asked.

"Yep. Apparently, I no longer work at Crawford Cereals. My mother wants me home."

Makay laughed. "Ha! That's the best news I've heard all week! Let's celebrate." She grabbed a spoon, scooped out a large portion of cookie dough, and handed it to me. "Hurray for freedom and pursuing your dreams."

"So you weren't even worried I'd go home?"

"Not on your life. You hate that place." She scooped more dough onto a second spoon and shoved it into my hand. "This is a two-spoon celebration."

Halla laughed and joined us, reaching for a spoon. "Me too!"

I was glad I'd gone to see Tessa first. Scaring Halla would have been inexcusable, especially with her father looming over us like some kind of terrifying phantom.

The ringing doorbell cut through our laughter. Immediately, Halla ran toward the bedroom. There, she'd be opening the sliding door, ready to go out onto the balcony and up onto the roof, just in case.

I set down my spoons and went to the door, peeking through the hole. A boy in a delivery uniform stood there with a vase of fuchsia lilies, bordered in white. "It's flowers," I whispered to Makay.

"Well, open it!" With Nate on one hip, she dragged the door open.

"I have a delivery for Lily Crawford?"

"There." Makay thumbed at me.

I signed his delivery pad and took the flowers. "Thank you."

I'd no sooner shut the door than Halla was out of the bedroom and peering over my shoulder. "Well? Who sent them?"

I was just as curious. There was only one man I'd been dating. I opened the envelope and removed the card, my heart doing funny little jumps as if it could already read what was inside.

Sorry, it read. *I was wrong. Please forgive me. Love, MJP. P.S. I hope lilies are still magic.*

"MJP," mused Halla. "That's Mario, right?"

I nodded. "Mario Jameson Perez."

Halla took a bite of dough from her spoon. "Something

tells me he didn't get the memo about you being just friends."

Makay found that hilarious. "That," she announced, "calls for even more cookie dough."

She was absolutely right.

The days flew by, with me having the time to complete many household tasks I'd been putting off because of work. Thursday morning, Halla stayed home again while Elsie worked with Ruth. After dropping off the girls, I drove to Teen Remake for my first official day on the job and attended the opening ceremony for the next Teen Nature that I would be helping out with on Friday and Saturday. The kids looked excited for the most part, some trying and failing to look bored. One girl kept staring at her father, as if she'd never seen him before, and I felt a rush of . . . envy? My father had never gone on any camping trip with me, and the fact that this father was here meant he was trying.

I was going to like it here.

Within forty minutes, they were on buses heading toward South Mountain. The rest of my four hours, I sat in group therapy sessions, which was apparently part of my training. It was a lot like my sessions on the roof with my girls, and before I could help myself, I was contributing as much as the therapist, a large black woman whose name was Jill.

As the kids filed from the room, Jill put her arm around my shoulders. "Lily, you're a natural. In another couple weeks, those girls will be telling you everything."

I grinned at her a bit sheepishly. "You're the one who's great with them. I think you'll have *me* telling you everything in the next few weeks."

Her laugh made me feel happy inside. "Oh, honey, we all have issues, and the more we can get them out, and talk about how we dealt with them, the more we can reach these kids. I know therapists will tell you that you need some distance, and it's true—for a therapist. But you're here to be like their big sister, at least with the girls. You just love them and leave the distance to me."

"That I think I can do."

"I know you can."

Jameson came in then and said, "Hey, can we borrow her for a video game contest?"

I was glad to see him, but there was no way I wanted to play today. "I'm not that good."

He grinned. "That's what I'm banking on. You'll be on the other team."

"What?"

"Trust me." The words spoke volumes.

"She can go," Jill said. "But she's only scheduled until twelve, so you be sure to let her go by then." To me, she added, "Now with the boys, you can leave a little distance, or they'll be flirting up a storm. They won't even mind if they lose to you." She gave a hearty laugh and waved us out the door.

Jameson took me to the room where I'd seen him playing before. A crowd of kids had gathered for the contest. "Two against two," Jameson explained. "The others are here to cheer us on."

His team player was a Hispanic boy, and my partner was a young man of indeterminate race. "Hey, sista," said the boy, offering me a fist bump. "I'm Felix. Don't you worry. After you get killed, I'll still beat 'em."

"Okay." I sat down on the couch, and the game began.

Jameson and his partner quickly ganged up on Felix, so I took my time learning the game. It wasn't all that different from the games I played with the girls, except instead of shooting everyone, you had to beat them by talking to teachers, doing service for needy bystanders, and preventing attacks on your competition by evil terrorists, all of which gave you points. You stopped your opponents from winning by asking them to help you perform different tasks, which they had to do, or lose points, and then while they were occupied, beating them to each kind deed.

While Jameson and his partner inundated Feliz with requests for service, I found my way through a maze to the mayor of the city and got permission to start a Feed the World campaign, saving a cat, an old man, and a little girl on the way. Then I went for the jugular and prevented attackers from taking out my competition with a toilet bomb. By the time Jameson realized what I was doing, I'd earned enough points to win the game.

"Way to go." Felix gave me another fist bump. "You like my game?"

"You made this? Yeah, I like it a lot."

Felix grinned. "I'll burn you a copy, and give you a link where you can send all your friends to buy it. It's gonna pay my way through college."

"You have to graduate high school first," Jameson reminded him.

"Yeah, yeah. You nag like my old man." We all laughed.

It was time for me to go, and Jameson had another group session, but he walked with me into the hallway. "Are we okay?" he asked.

I'd texted him a thanks for the flowers, but we hadn't talked since. Two long, torturous days. "Yeah. Fine."

"Good, because I've been wanting to ask—would you like to come to Sunday dinner at my parents'?"

His parents? Before I had too much time to get excited, my logical self kicked in. "Wait, doesn't your family live in Tucson? That's what, about a two-hour drive?"

"Yeah. So it's really a full day, not just dinner. I don't go home that often, but I sort of mentioned you to my mother, and she's been after me to invite you."

I wondered if this was before or after our argument Friday night. Still, he *had* talked to his mother about me, and excitement over that vied with my reluctance to leave the girls. My mind raced over the possibilities. But in the end, I knew it wasn't going to work. "You know, it sounds fun, but with the weekend hours here and looking for a new job, I won't be spending as much time with the girls, except on Sunday, and I can't leave them all day." Can't, meaning I didn't want to.

"Oh, didn't I say?" His smile widened and his eyes gleamed with his customary amusement. "They're invited—in fact, my mother would have my hide if I didn't bring them. Payden's coming with me, and I was thinking of borrowing his mother's van to fit us all."

"You sure your mom wants all of us?" My mother would be throwing a fit. It was one thing to call a caterer for her elegant dinner parties, but quite another to feed runaway girls.

"You kidding? My mom loves to cook, and she's used to doing large amounts." He gazed at me with his head titled to the side, an expression on his face that was both pleading and hopeful. "Please come?"

"I'll talk to the girls."

"Great. They'll so want to come." He took a few steps back into the room where the teens were sitting in a circle on the carpet. "Make sure you tell them I have two really good-looking brothers in high school."

I laughed. "Okay."

I watched him turn and join the circle of kids. There was no counselor, and that told me he'd completed whatever hours were required for him to run this session alone. Would that be me someday? I hoped so because it was a lot more interesting than making sure cereal packers met their daily quotas.

"I can't believe he's taking you home to meet his mommy," Saffron teased as Ruth and Elsie darted inside the apartment to inform us that Jameson had arrived in his borrowed van.

"You sure you won't go with us?" I asked Saffron.

"Nope, I'm sort of away from that whole family

dinner thing right now, no matter how cool the family. It would be different if you weren't just friends, but why should I waste my time if he's not going to be around in a few months?" She winked and flashed me a grin. "Don't worry. I'm going to hang out with Russ instead, but I don't like him enough to get into trouble. We're just friends."

"Friends with kissing benefits," Zoey shot back, with more than a little envy in her voice. Zoey might try to hide herself with pounds, but like every other girl, she dreamed about having a boyfriend who really loved her.

Saffron laughed. "Yep. It's a beautiful relationship."

"Just friends" was Saffron's way of protecting herself. That worked fine for now, given her age, but someday, she'd need to get beyond what happened to her—with her family and with losing the baby. I planned to learn enough before then to help her when that time came.

Saffron grabbed the bags of snacks I'd put together and passed them to me. "Have fun, you guys."

"You too," I said.

The rest of the girls and I thundered down the stairs, Halla in her wig and Ruth in her boy clothes. At least Elsie's hair was brushed. That was some progress. We met Jameson on the second-floor landing, just as our neighbor was coming out for a smoke. The neighbor's face was dark with stubble, and on one of his arms was a tattoo of a dragon.

Elsie noticed him and buried her face into me as we passed. The reaction wasn't missed by Jameson. "Is that the neighbor you told me about?" he asked in a low voice when we reached the last stair.

The girls had already started across the parking lot to the van, where Payden had opened the side door for them, too far away to hear us. "Yes—the one who freaked Elsie out last week. I don't even know his name."

"Maybe you should report him to the management."

"For what, smoking? Besides, I'm too worried he's been taking notes on how many girls I have living with me. My lease says up to three people for the one-bedroom apartments, and I just had my landlord sign the foster parent form that says he's aware that Zoey and Bianca are living here." I sighed. "The landlord might not even care about the others. At least, he hasn't said anything, and there are a bunch of people here who don't follow that rule. I swear, one family here has like twenty-five relatives in a two-bedroom apartment. But if DCS ever talks to him, I don't want him to know anything officially."

Jameson glanced up at the second floor, where my neighbor was no longer in sight. Maybe he hadn't been coming out for a smoke but to see what was making noise on the metal stairs. "We should look him up on the child predator list. They have one, you know. But what you really need is to move. I've been looking up different places. I hope you don't mind."

"I don't." We'd reached the front of the van. "But I'll probably need to find a second job first. I'm no longer working for my dad."

He stopped walking. "You're not?"

I didn't want to vilify my parents, though part of me felt they deserved it. "We came to the mutual conclusion that I wasn't going to work there anymore."

"Good for you."

When I raised my brows in puzzlement, he added, "You hated it there."

"How come everyone seems to know that? It's not as if I complained."

"I can just tell—your eyes are different when you talk about the factory. Look, it'll work out. I'll help you find a place you can afford."

I gave a gentle snort.

He laughed. "Did you just snort?"

"Um, no. Maybe. I just think you're biting off more than you realize."

"Hey, I've got connections."

"Well, I'm going to need more than just an apartment at the rate I'm picking up girls. I seem to get at least one on every major holiday."

"Wow, if I used the term 'picking up girls' like that, someone would put me in jail."

I snorted loudly this time. "Yes, it was a snort. You're funny."

Again the deliberate grin that sent delicious heat through my belly. "Good. I like to see you smile."

His dark eyes held mine, and the heat spread through my limbs. I felt rooted to the spot, held by his gaze. His face shouldn't be so familiar to me, but it was. For several heartbeats we stood there, as if at the mouth of a raging river—and I wanted more than anything to jump inside and get wet, without worrying about drowning. Before meeting him, I'd been so careful with my plans, my feelings. Maybe I was a lot like Saffron, holding back because of the love I'd been denied as a child. Yet I'd had Tessa, then Makay and the girls, and here was Jameson, staring at me like he'd never seen a woman before.

Was this how the beginning of love felt? I didn't know because it was certainly the first time I'd ever experienced it.

If only so much didn't ride on trusting him.

The sliding door on the van opened. "Hey, are we going or not?" Payden asked. "It's already getting a little stuffy in here."

"Right."

The connection broken, I hurried toward Payden's sliding door, but Jameson sprinted after me and opened the front passenger door instead. "You're riding here with me," he said, offering me a hand up. "If that's okay."

I nodded and took his hand. His touch felt warm and comfortable and exhilarating. I wanted more. More of him. More than friendship.

He tipped forward, brushing a kiss over my lips. It was all I could do not to grab him and kiss him again.

"I hope you're ready for this," he said. "My family can get loud."

I glanced toward the two rows of back seats, where Zoey and Halla were arguing about bands as Ruth tried to play peacemaker. "You're kidding, right?"

"Nope. You haven't seen anything yet."

12

The supposed two-hour trip took an extra half hour with all the potty breaks, and the girls and their tiny bladders became a joke between Jameson and Payden. Between the stops, we sang along with CDs and played the alphabet game, which the girls claimed Jameson and Payden cheated at by using the gas line warning signs. The warnings were periodically pasted on wooden posts along the roads, and the men couldn't possibly see the letters they alleged were there. But by the end of the trip, the girls were also using the signs, skipping all the way from A through J, or L through P, or R through W. Only the K, Q, X, Y, and Z were missing from the sign and had to be found elsewhere. They went through the alphabet dozens of times before they finally grew bored.

We pulled up at his parents' house, which was a squat, stuccoed affair. The whole thing could almost fit into the kitchen and family room of my parents' house. Shaking the image from my head, I followed Jameson up the walk and waited as he knocked on the front door. It swung open to reveal a teenage version of Jameson.

The boy hugged his brother and blushed as he was introduced as Tim. "Come on in," he invited. "Everyone's in here."

I wouldn't be my mother's daughter if I didn't notice the outdated wallpaper and the short, emerald green carpet in the living room that might have been popular in the 1990s. Tim led us through the room to the kitchen, which had to be the largest space in the house but was barely able to fit a long wooden table. The kitchen ceiling had boxes of fluorescent lighting that would have my mother shaking her head, but to me it felt just right. There was no mistaking the sense of coziness here.

The kitchen connected with a small family room that was set down a couple feet, separated from the kitchen by a few stairs. Most of Jameson's family were gathered there, and at least three different board games were in play. A TV also blared, but nobody appeared to be watching it.

A woman I assumed was Jameson's mother turned from the sink. "Ah, you're here," she said, drying her hands before hugging him. She was of average height and weight, with dark blond hair, blue eyes, and a smile that put me at ease.

"You must be Lily," she said. "My son goes on and on about you. Your eyes, how good you are with the girls. I am so pleased to meet you. I'm Heidi."

"Uh, Mom," Jameson said. She laughed as he quickly began introducing the girls.

"Are you guys hungry?" Heidi asked when he was finished. "Dinner won't be ready for several hours yet, but I have some chips and stuff on the table." She gestured to the table, which was covered with clear plastic. The legs were intricately carved, and the surface gleamed even beneath the plastic. Now this piece of furniture my mother would covet. "Please, help yourselves."

"Thanks," I said, "but all we've been doing for the past two hours is eating. Jameson and I both brought too many snacks for the trip."

Her laugh once again filled the kitchen. "You call him Jameson? Good choice."

I wanted to say that mothers were always right, but it wasn't true, or my girls wouldn't be with me, and I'd be in Flagstaff right now. "He looks like a Jameson. I hope that's okay."

"Oh, I don't mind sharing it with you. It means you're on my side." She winked at me to show she was kidding as she hooked her arm around one of mine. "Let's go meet the rest of the clan."

We crossed the kitchen and went down the three steps into the family room, where Jameson's family had stopped the games they were playing and stared, a sea of interested brown eyes. Heidi released me and started the introductions, her hands moving in front of her in sign language as she presented her husband, Antonio, and their children Linda, Robert, Eric, and Angela. "You met Tim already," she added. I knew from Jameson that the three oldest after him—Linda, Tim, and Robert—were each a year apart, eighteen, seventeen, and sixteen, coming like a flood after five years of Jameson being an only child. Eric was twelve, and Angela ten. What he hadn't told me was that Angela was deaf.

As the family members were introduced, each spoke and signed their greetings. When the girls or I responded,

Jameson or one of the others translated our speech. It was a beautiful thing, the ease with which they spoke and signed simultaneously, and for several minutes I found it difficult to look past their hands. Angela was the only light-haired Perez, taking after her mother, but her eyes were definitely her father's. Antonio Perez had black hair sprinkled liberally with gray and was a foot shorter than Jameson. He was handsome with a sort of European flare that reminded me of vampire movies.

"Come play with us!" Eric demanded. "We can play *Bang!* But at the table because there's more room."

Heidi leaned over and turned off the television. "Oh," she said, sighing with relief. "That's so much better."

The girls didn't know what *Bang!* was, but the Perez kids were eager teachers, and soon they were at the large kitchen table firing bullets, playing misses, and using their alcohol cards to gain life points as outlaws, deputies, and renegades had a shoot-out to the death.

Jameson didn't join the game but knelt between a beautiful checkered coffee table and his youngest sister, who had remained on the couch. Her arms and hands moved at light speed as she talked to her brother.

"What's she saying?" I asked.

"That you're pretty." He signed as he spoke. "That your eyes are kind. And some other stuff I'm not translating because it's embarrassing." Angela laughed at that.

I reached into the only experience I had with sign language—a single season viewing of *Switched at Birth*—and told her thank you.

She grinned and signed something before hopping up and running into the kitchen to watch her family play the card game. "She says 'you're welcome,'" Jameson said, rising from the carpet.

"I figured. Why didn't you tell me?"

"What? That she's deaf?" He shrugged. "Honestly, I didn't even think about it. Not until we arrived, and I saw you guys watching my mother sign. Angela's been deaf all her life. We all learned ASL because we wanted to be a real part of her world. It's an entire unique community. Even Payden and my aunt learned. It was kind of funny because my father picked it up better than he has English."

Tears choked me. Because if Angela had been born in my family, I couldn't say that my parents would have reacted the same way. She would have more likely been hidden from view, maybe institutionalized. "I like that you know sign language." In fact, I liked it a lot. "Will you teach me?"

He nodded and signed "Yes," another of the few signs I recognized.

"What about Spanish? Do you know that too?"

"Not as well as ASL. My mother speaks Spanish too, and my parents tried to teach me when I was young, before I began school. My grandparents would also come to visit, and I spent a summer in Spain with them when I was seventeen. But I'm not as good as I should be, and none of my other siblings, except Linda, speak it at all. With my mom being American, and my dad kind of quiet, it was just too hard to keep it up."

I wondered what else I didn't know about him. "Guess it's strange to have the last name Perez and not speak Spanish."

He laughed. "It happens a lot around these parts."

The Perez household was louder than I expected, even after Jameson's warning, but the girls were having a great time. There was no awkwardness that wasn't immediately laughed away. At dinner, all fifteen of us fit around the table, with one spot to spare. After a blessing on the meal, everyone raced for the food, and when I was slow, Jameson began filling my plate.

"Around here it's who can grab the best food first," he said. My girls already seemed to know that, and they beat even the Perezes for seconds.

After dinner, Antonio and Jameson took me to see Antonio's garage-turned-shop. He was working on a bookcase, a fireplace mantle, and another dining table like the one he'd made for his family.

"Your work is amazing," I said.

"I don't make lot of money," he responded in heavily accented English. "But I am happy, and it is honest work. I have been home these past ten years with Angela."

I knew I shouldn't be jealous of a little girl for having a father who wanted to be home with her, but for a moment, I felt very much alone as I recalled my relationship with my own father. "I think that's perfect."

Antonio grinned and gave me a wink. "If you stick around, eh? One day I make you a table."

"Well, I'm going to have a big house with a ton of foster girls who will probably ruin it."

He laughed. "Oh, yes. Good. Happy house. Lots of children. A big table is what they need. For now"—he picked up a pair of bookends from a table full of similar ones—"you have this."

The entwined pair of cheetahs was decidedly heavy. "Oh, it's beautiful, but you can't—"

"We sell them at craft fairs," he said. "They are easy to make."

"Our bread and butter," Jameson explained. "My mother sells them while he finishes the big pieces."

"How did you learn to work with wood? Who taught you?" I asked Antonio.

"My father and grandfather. I no think it was for me, and for a long time I denied the call, but it finally found me." His words reminded me of what Jameson said about his father leaving his accounting job.

"Mario is also an artist," Antonio said. "Once I thought he would follow my footsteps, but now he follows my first profession." His smile showed he didn't care.

I looked at Jameson. "Will you show me something you made?"

"The coffee table," Antonio said.

"The one with different colors of wood on the top? Wow, I'm impressed."

Jameson groaned. "Just don't look too closely. Angela can do better, and she's only ten."

At that, Antonio looked proud. "She only lacks strength, but she feels the wood. In here, I wear earplugs. She does not hear the saw. We make a perfect pair."

We all laughed and returned to the house, with me clutching my new bookends. The noise hit us again in a wave, but I was more used to it now.

I made a dash to the coffee table for a second look.

Squatting next to it, I could see a few places where the joined wood was beginning to separate slightly, but it was still beautiful. "Very nice."

Jameson shrugged but looked pleased. "It's okay."

"Your family is nice." I ran a hand idly over the coffee table. "Thank you for bringing me."

Jameson stood with his hands in his pockets. "I wanted you to see where I'm from, and I wanted you to meet them." He glanced into the kitchen, where the kids were playing a round of Skip-Bo. "They are a big part of me."

"I can see that." I wondered if he knew how lucky he was. I did—and being here changed the way I felt about him. I still wanted him, he was still attractive to me, but now there was an added depth, one I couldn't resist.

I looked down at the coffee table to hide the tears seeping into my eyes. He must have sensed something because he squatted beside me. "What is it?"

"I have this dream," I said. "A big house with all the girls. There's lots of laughter, music, and even a dog."

"A dog?"

"Yeah." All weekend, Elsie had talked non-stop about the dogs she and Ruth had walked on Thursday and Saturday, and seeing her come alive made a dog a permanent part of my dream house.

I risked a glance and found his mouth curved into a smile. "And there's chaos, messes, and sometimes fighting, but most of the time there's just a sense of . . . family, even for strangers. That's what you have here, and it's really . . . good."

"I'm glad you think so." He put his hand over mine, and this time his touch caused an ache inside me that I couldn't name.

"You should know that my family is nothing like this," I felt compelled to say. "My sister is great, but you saw my mother, and . . . I don't even know my father."

"That's okay. In that house of yours, you can do it any way you want. You don't have to do what they did."

"Dessert!" Heidi called from the kitchen. "Hurry and get it. It's starting to get dark and you guys need to get going."

"She hates me leaving in the dark," Jameson said. "I don't think she's realized that it's going to be dark before we get back to Phoenix, however fast we get out of here."

Laughing, we hurried over to the table for large slices of double-layer chocolate cake with whipped raspberry filling. This time I found myself at the counter with the wall on my left and Payden on my right. For the first time since our arrival, he was away from Elsie, who was separated from him by Angela.

He leaned over in my direction. "Lily, I need to talk to you about something."

The seriousness of his voice made me put down my fork. "What?"

"A guy came to the store asking questions. He put up these." He passed me a folded sheet, which I started to open.

His hand shot out to stop me, but not before I caught the slightest glimpse of Elsie's face on the paper. "Not here. She'll see. I didn't tell him anything, of course, but one of the other clerks remembered seeing Elsie. You can't bring her to the store anymore." He glanced over to where Elsie and Angela were busy writing notes to each other and giggling, though I'd learned that Angela was fairly adept at reading lips. "I'm sorry," Payden added.

My stomach had fallen with that glimpse of Elsie's picture. First the Internet plea to find Halla and now flyers of Elsie. "Thank you," I said mechanically. "I'll take care of it."

Payden nodded, staring down at his cake as though he'd lost his appetite. My own cake had no flavor, but I forked up a mouthful anyway. What was I going to do?

Feeling eyes on me, I turned to see Jameson at the table, wedged between his father and his brother Tim. There was a question in his eyes. "Later," I mouthed.

Somehow I finished the cake and said goodbye to Jameson's family without puking or bursting into angry tears. Heidi hugged me as I left, whispering in my ear. "You're everything he said and more. I hope you'll come see us again."

"Thank you. I will."

As the girls piled into the van, Jameson pulled me aside. "What was on that paper? Payden's not in trouble, is he?"

Wordlessly, I handed it to him, and he opened it, shock immediately registering on his face. "Oh, no." I was glad his back was to his parents, who stood at the door to wave goodbye.

"She ran away at least five and a half or six weeks ago," I said. "Maybe more. She's been with me for more than a month of that time, and there's been nothing like this before. Why now?"

"I don't know. But this says her father's from Tempe. All his contact info is here."

I took back the flyer. "I knew she had to be from somewhere in Arizona from the comments she's made, but Tempe is so close. I . . . these flyers are going to make it impossible for her to go anywhere. And one of the clerks at Payden's store already identified her."

"I'm so sorry."

"'Missing and endangered,' it says. So what do you think? Could he have thought she'd come back, and when she didn't, he finally put out flyers?"

"Possibly."

"What should I do?"

His jaw tightened with resolve. "We'll think of something."

The weeks flew by with me working to keep everything together. Halla started going with Ruth again
to work, using her wig, and Elsie didn't leave the house,
except to Makay's or on errands with me at night in the
car. We spent a lot of time on the roof once the heat of the
day had eased enough to make it tolerable. I also finished
the rest of my foster parent training.

For the first time in my life, work was a welcome
distraction. I loved being with the kids at Teen Remake,
especially on my full Friday at Teen Nature, where I
worked from noon to ten. Makay was with Elsie and the
girls, so I didn't worry about them, and seeing Jameson at
the camp was a plus. Though we didn't have much time
for privacy, we did steal a few kisses under the moonlight
at the camp before I headed home.

I was falling for him, I had no doubt about that. I only
hoped he felt the same way.

During the days or evenings we didn't have work,
Jameson was with me and the girls, watching more
than our fair share of videos, playing games, or making

something in the kitchen. He'd taken to bringing groceries, and somewhat guiltily, I let him. Between my last paycheck from the factory and a gift from Tessa, I'd paid June's rent and our utilities. We were scraping by on food, even with Jameson's help and Payden's offerings, but we would be getting funds from DCS soon, and I expected a paycheck from Teen Remake any day.

Most nights we tried to kick Jameson out before midnight because I worried that DCS would somehow find out and think he was living with us and take Zoey and Bianca away. Since the girls were finally out of school, we could sleep in many mornings, but there were still Ruth and Halla's errands, and Saffron, who woke us up every day with her blow dryer as she got ready for work.

The knock we'd feared on the door hadn't come yet, though the flyers of Elsie were plastered everywhere. I began to hope it would all die down.

Some three weeks after our visit to his family, Jameson came into one of my Thursday morning sessions with Jill and asked to see me. Jill smiled knowingly, and the girls in our session tittered.

My face flushed, and that made them laugh harder. "Be quick about it," Jill said, grinning.

"What's this about?" I asked as Jameson pulled me into an empty room.

He didn't answer, his lips closing the distance between us, and for the next few blissful moments, I let myself become lost in his touch. When we broke apart, he was smiling and so was I.

"I don't think they're paying us to make out," I whispered.

"No, but I had an idea last night, about Ruth. It was something you mentioned that social worker said when she came to your apartment, and why you keep kicking me out every night so early. I didn't want to get your hopes up, but my hunch panned out."

"What hunch?"

"That guy Ruth's mother has living with her? Tyron Fisher? Well, I asked Bea to look him up through her connections with the police department. Turns out, he did time for rape."

I stared at him. "What?"

"Yes. And get this, the girl was only sixteen. There's no way DCS would place a child in any house he was living in."

"Can it be that easy?" Goose bumps rippled up my bare arms.

"Hard to believe, but I think so."

"What if Ruth's mother dumps him when she finds out she's losing her extra food stamps?"

"That's where Bea comes in. She can feel her out just like you did, and once she determines that Ruth's mother will likely do it again . . ."

"But they've interviewed her before—several times. After the first time, she just got another boyfriend, and he assaulted Ruth too."

"Bea's more determined than whoever had the case before. I think we should trust her."

I hesitated. Jameson was making a lot of sense, but it was still hard for me. Ruth had been through too much already.

Jameson's smile was nervous. "The worst that can

happen is they send her home, and she runs away again. Ruth's mother only wants the food stamps, right?"

"And to clean her house, I think. Ruth's the only one of my girls who does her chores without me riding her."

"Good." Jameson smirked. "I might have had something to do with that."

"What?"

"Yeah, remember that first day we met? While you were getting ready for work, I told Ruth and Halla I'd give them ten bucks if they'd make sure your place was clean when you got home."

I gaped. "It was. I remember being surprised. Please don't tell me you're still paying them."

"Oh, no, but I do bring Ruth a box of toaster tarts a couple times a week. She loves that junk."

"That would explain the boxes I keep finding stashed behind the couch. I thought she was hoarding food again."

"She probably is hoarding them," he said with a grin, "but I hoard chocolate-covered cinnamon bears and you hoard croissants, so who cares? Anyway, if she gets sent home, we tell her not to clean and to eat a lot. That way her mother won't care when she runs. I really don't think it will go that far, but by then you'll have a new apartment. The point is she'll be safe from the boyfriend. Besides, once Bea knows Ruth was assaulted, she won't send her back if there's a chance it'll happen again."

He waited, and I knew it was my decision.

Jameson cared about Ruth, and I'd seen her blossom these past three weeks under his care. He'd even helped me with her new hairstyle that had turned out quite well.

Ruth trusted him so much that she hardly ever wore her boy clothes anymore when he was around, and that was becoming a problem because we didn't have enough clothes to fit her long legs.

"Okay," I said.

Jameson didn't wait for me to change my mind. "Good. Bea's gone back to DCS, but I'll ask if she can come talk with you after you get off. I'll have a session at that time, though. Can you do it alone?"

"Yeah."

He kissed me again, his hands around my back, pushing me closer until I felt I would melt into him. It was all I could do to pull myself away. We'd have to decide what to do about us soon because I wanted him as much as he wanted me, but a casual relationship was out of the question—just like alcohol and staying out too late. The girls watched our every move, and they knew me too well for me to keep secrets. Besides, what I felt for Jameson went far beyond casual.

He could break my heart.

"So how long has she been with you?" Bea wasn't smiling after my hurried explanation about Ruth.

"Since last Thanksgiving."

"So before Zoey and Bianca."

I nodded.

"Why didn't you tell me about her?"

"Because DCS sent her back twice before, and she can't go through that again."

Bea frowned. "Well, it's been six months, and her mother hasn't reported her missing. So I'd say that woman is in a world of trouble already. She might have gotten away with it if she didn't have that man there, but I think I can ask just the right questions to give enough doubt. I will have to contact the former caseworker on this, though. I want to see if they properly documented her abuse, and why there wasn't adequate follow up."

"Thank you."

"You're going to have to find a new place to live," Bea said as I headed for the door. "Especially at the rate you're finding girls."

She didn't know the half of it.

"Is there anything else you're not telling me?" she asked.

"No, but I can't wait until you meet Ruth. She has your hair."

Friday and Saturday morning passed with no word from Bea. I came home from my Saturday morning shift at Teen Nature worried that no news was bad news. I hadn't dared tell Ruth anything for fear I'd scare her.

I was scared enough for both of us.

I busied myself with washing our clothes at the Laundromat and getting the girls to clean the apartment. When night fell, we still had a mound of clothes on the couch, and Halla's and Ruth's beds were laid out in preparation for our movie fest.

Halla and Ruth volunteered to pick up our Saturday

night videos. "Come with us, Elsie," Ruth said. "It's dark and you can wear my hat. No one will see you."

Elsie hesitated, looking at me. "It'll be okay," I said. "Just use my hoodie." She nodded with a smile that told me she was growing stir-crazy sitting inside all day.

"You guys coming?" Halla asked Zoey and Bianca.

"No, we'll stay and help get rid of these clothes so we have somewhere to sit." Zoey thumbed at the couch, and I felt a little rush of pride that she was thinking of me. I only hoped Jameson wasn't bribing her with toaster tarts.

"And I'll make popcorn," Bianca added.

I gave Halla my credit card. "Three movies only," I told her. "Don't go inside for snacks."

She grinned. "We don't need 'em. Your *friend* who is a boy but not your *boyfriend* will bring some." Giggling, they left the apartment.

They'd only been gone a few minutes when the doorbell rang. Bianca ran to look through the peephole, while Zoey and I froze. Bianca turned back to me. "It's the landlord. He's got a guy with him. Never seen him before."

A few minutes earlier, I would have sent the girls to the roof, and now I didn't know if it was good or bad that they were out in the street. I turned to Zoey. "If it's someone looking for the girls, you go warn them not to come back, okay? Tell them to go to the park, to our meeting place."

She nodded, her eyes frightened the way they'd been when I'd first found her at that same park.

"But first fold up those two beds. Quick!" I didn't want the men thinking we had more than us sleeping here.

"Dump the blankets on the other side of the couch. Then just sit and watch television or something until you can get past them." Saffron was still home, in the bathroom, getting ready for a date, but there was no warning her now. At least she wasn't at risk like the others, and she knew well enough to keep her mouth shut.

Pounding on the door sent my heart into overdrive. I wished Jameson was here. "I'm coming," I called to the men. "Just wait a moment." Glancing at Zoey and Bianca, I was relieved to see they'd already folded the chair-beds and were sitting on them, the television on.

I opened the door to the landlord, a short, thin man about my own age with a blond scruff of a goatee that made him look five years younger. Rumors had it he was the son of the owner, and I suspected it was true because he lacked the ability to fix anything. No one would ever hire a non-relative so inept.

"Sorry," I said with false brightness. "I'm in the middle of laundry, as you can see, and I don't let my girls open the door in this neighborhood." I gave the landlord a bland smile at my not-so-subtle dig. "May I help you?"

The man with the landlord craned his neck to see past me, obviously not content with his limited view of the girls. "She's got to be here. That guy downstairs swears she is."

"What are you talking about?" But I knew, because the stranger looked like Elsie. He had the same dark curly hair and soulful brown eyes—he was gorgeous in every sense of the word. But his unsmiling mouth had a cruel, demanding twist that was missing in Elsie's sweet face.

The landlord said, "Mr. Reynolds here is looking for his daughter. Her name is Elsie. Do you mind if we come in?"

"We were just about ready to go out for some videos. Is there a problem?"

"We need to search your apartment," Mr. Reynolds said, his voice staccato and sharp. "I know you're hiding her!"

"What? Are you crazy? Maybe I should call the police."

"Maybe you should," he retorted. "Because I'm not leaving until I find her."

"I don't know who you're talking about. There's no one here but us." I glanced back at Zoey and Bianca, who stared at me with wide, frightened eyes.

"I'll see for myself." Mr. Reynolds pushed past me, forcing his way into the apartment.

"You can't do this!" I shouted. "Look, you're scaring my girls."

"She's right, sir," said the landlord, who stayed nervously in the hall. "You need a warrant."

"I don't need anything. She's *my* daughter!"

"I'm calling the police." I ran for my phone in my purse on the kitchen counter, but Elsie's father was already heading down the hallway to the bedroom. I watched helplessly as he opened the door. The three beds there could be for Zoey, Bianca, and me, but would he see anything he recognized as Elsie's? Had she taken her pink backpack with her? She'd worn it everywhere at first, but she didn't anymore.

Pushing open the door, Reynolds stared inside while

my heart panicked so much that I couldn't drag in a breath. My head began to buzz.

He turned back to me, coming fast down the hall, and my laboring heart couldn't even feel relief that he hadn't found anything. "Where is she?" he demanded. I had the sense that if the landlord hadn't come hesitantly into the apartment, Elsie's father would have shoved me up against the wall.

"There's no one here but us," I repeated. "You've got the wrong apartment."

At that moment, a sound came from the bathroom. Triumph filling his face, Reynolds reached for the door, just as Saffron opened it. "What is going on out here?" She looked from me to Elsie's father and back again.

I started to talk, but Elsie's father beat me to it. "I'm looking for Elsie."

Saffron shrugged. "Sorry, I don't know anyone by that name. I'm just here visiting my friend." She gestured to Zoey, who had come to stand by me. Why was she still here instead of warning Elsie?

"Girl," Saffron added, "if this is what goes on here, next time we should hang out at my house."

"So you don't know my daughter?" Reynolds shoved a picture under her nose.

"Sorry. Cute kid, though."

"Can I see that?" I took the picture from his unwilling hand. Sure enough, it was a younger Elsie, smiling sadly at the camera. My heart ached for her. "Sorry," I said.

"You're sure?" Reynolds was backing down now. Finally. "Show it to her." He pointed at Zoey.

Zoey pretended to study it. "No. And I don't recognize

her from school either. If it was that guy downstairs who said she was here, well, he's a perv. He's always staring at my little sister. She has dark hair too. He probably just wants a reward." To me, her voice sounded strained, but Elsie's father couldn't know that. He wasn't blind, though. With her darker skin, anyone could see Bianca didn't resemble Elsie in the least. No way could the neighbor be confused.

Except that Bianca was no longer in the apartment for Elsie's father to compare.

"Well, call me if you hear anything." No apology or "please." Grabbing his picture from Zoey, Reynolds fished a flyer from his pocket and thrust it in my direction. It was identical to the one Payden had given me.

"How long has she been missing?" I made myself ask.

"A couple weeks." He didn't look at me as he told the lie, but started for the door.

"Sorry about this," the landlord said in an undertone as Elsie's father exited the apartment. "I didn't expect him to go all ballistic like that. And I didn't think it would hurt to ask if you'd seen her since you seem to have a lot of girls running in and out all the time."

I dredged up a smile. "Zoey and Bianca have a lot of girlfriends, that's all."

He stepped outside, and I shut the door with relief.

What now?

Obviously, our downstairs neighbor had recognized Elsie from the flyers and had called the number. I was grateful Mr. Reynolds had come here himself and not with the police because they would have probably been more thorough, maybe even holding me here until they received a warrant to search through our things, including my phone with the pictures I'd taken of the girls. I needed to remove the photos, maybe ask Jameson to store them on his computer. Because I knew it was only a matter of time until Elsie's father returned, this time with the police. The downstairs neighbor wouldn't be the only tenant here who would remember seeing Elsie. The police could also search the camera feeds at the nearby convenience stores or traffic lights, and no matter how careful we'd been in the past few weeks, they'd identify Elsie and connect her to us.

I had to take her somewhere safe.

"Bianca?" I asked Zoey.

"I told her to meet the girls. He looked like he might start hitting you." Zoey wasn't much for physical affection, but she hugged me now. "I couldn't leave."

I understood. Of course she couldn't. Just like she hadn't been able to leave Bianca with her uncle.

"Interesting that he only started searching for Elsie a few weeks ago," Saffron said. "After all the bruising would be gone. I bet he knows how long they take to fade."

Which meant the last time he'd beaten Elsie hadn't been the first. No wonder she was so frightened.

"We have to get out of here!" Zoey said.

"Not all of us." My mind raced. "You two and Bianca can stay here with Makay. I'll go to Tessa's with the others. Just temporarily. We'll figure it out."

"What about tonight?" Zoey looked ready to cry, and I knew it wasn't because of the DVDs. She was scared for Elsie, because of what she herself had endured.

"Let's all go to Tessa's. We'll talk about it there."

"Uh, I still have my date with Russ," Saffron said. "But he's taking me to start service on my phone, now that I can pay for it, and I'll call you and give you the number so you can tell me what you've decided. Meanwhile, I can stay here with Makay to watch the apartment. I'm not scared."

It was the start of a plan. Impulsively, I leaned over to hug Saffron. "Thanks for keeping it cool there. You did great." I reached to pull Zoey into our embrace. "Both of you."

"That's what family's for," Saffron said. "And you guys are mine." Zoey nodded forcefully.

"Which reminds me," Saffron added, "Makay and I've been working on something with Russ for Halla's dad. I think I'm almost ready to show you."

My mind could only hold one trauma at a time, but I trusted Makay to make sure Saffron abided by my stipulations. "Okay, good. But help me gather up some stuff for the girls tonight. Just a couple things in some of my big handbags. In case they're watching."

14

Tessa's two roommates were out, so no one objected to our arrival. Tessa, who'd canceled a date, met us at the door. "I'm sorry to make you stay in on one of your only nights off from the factory," I said.

She waved my words aside. "That's okay. Come on in."

"We brought videos."

"Great."

My phone buzzed. I knew it was Jameson again. He'd already texted three times when I canceled the movie night, and he was still waiting for an explanation. His concern made me feel slightly weepy.

Tessa saw my face. "Is that the mysterious boyfriend I still haven't met?"

"Maybe. I've got to call him."

"You should invite him over. No reason not to."

I took my arm from Elsie, who hadn't said a word since I'd picked her up at the park but had cried silent tears. "Honey, I'm going to talk to Jameson, okay? My sister will stay right with you. Don't worry. You're safe here." I wasn't really sure how long that would be true.

Elsie didn't respond, but she let Tessa take her hand and lead her into their family room.

I called Jameson. "Sorry," I said. "It's been crazy." Despite my attempt at control, my voice broke on the last word.

"What happened?"

I started a rundown, but he stopped me as I described how Elsie's father had pushed inside the apartment and screamed at us. "Did he hurt you?"

"No. Just scared us all. Elsie was with the girls getting videos, and it's not that far—I was afraid she'd come home when he was still there. If she'd been home when he'd come, I'd have sent her to the roof. He was like a madman. I don't know what to do."

"Where are you now? Not still at the park, I hope."

"No, we're at my sister's."

"Well, that's good. They won't know that address, at least until they figure out you're related."

My heart plummeted. "I put Tessa's address on my employee papers for Teen Remake. I didn't trust that Bea would figure out things for Zoey and Bianca."

"Then we'll have to tell Bea. She's the only one who'll be able to do anything. Elsie's father is sure to go to the police, and they'll identify Elsie and find you. There's no way they won't. If we come forward and show Bea those pictures you took when you found her, we'll at least have a chance." He paused before adding, "And some follow-up on her case, if it doesn't work out."

I remembered how on the roof Elsie had said she'd rather die than go back. I was failing her, and I didn't know how to turn it around.

"I can call her if you want," he said. "But either way, you should stay there through the weekend."

"Okay."

"Can I come over?"

"Please."

"Text me the address. I'll be right there."

I'd no sooner rejoined the girls than Saffron called my cell phone. "Okay," she announced. "This is my new number. I'm official. I can't believe I finally have a phone again."

"Congratulations."

"It gets better," she said. "I don't know if it's going to work, but Makay, Russ, and I are fighting Halla's dad right this minute online—with some other people too. Hurry and go look at his Go Fund Me. And before you ask, none of the posts can be traced back to me. For the past few weeks we've been using Russ's old laptop at a restaurant with free Wi-Fi to talk to a group of people who fight abuse. There's a lot of girls in the group, former victims. Anyway, Makay helped us track down some of that information Jameson gave you, and we turned it over to them—all anonymously, of course—and they checked it out. So now they're posting about it. You've got to see it!"

I ran for my laptop that was in one of my bags, motioning for the girls to gather around. "I'm putting you on speaker," I told Saffron. "What was that URL?"

When the Go Fund Me site came up, there were hundreds of comments, all of them negative about Halla's father. "You gave your daughter only broccoli and water for two weeks after she refused to eat her broccoli,"

Ruth read. "I think a sixteen-year-old should decide if she wants carrots instead of broccoli."

I skimmed ahead, reading snippets to myself. ". . . made her miss school for a month after a boy called the house . . . heard about the donation you gave to your priest . . . is that why he didn't tell the police your daughter went to him? School officials have repeatedly visited your house . . . sixteen is old enough for emancipation . . . she's taken care of herself for almost seven months without you . . . leave her alone . . . won't let her use the phone . . . threw out all her clothes . . . told your wife not to talk to the neighbors . . . living on bread and water . . . weighed only ninety pounds after you handcuffed her to the bed for six months . . . finally jumped from the window to kill herself to end the pain . . . broke her arm . . . ran away from the hospital when they said she had to go home . . . living on the street better than locked away . . . shame on you for abusing that poor girl . . . you are abusive and insane . . . scamming money from good people."

That was only the beginning. There were hundreds of comments.

Tessa made a sound in her throat. "I can't believe it!"

"It's all true," Halla said in a small voice.

"Oh, honey, I know that." Tessa hugged her. "I just meant all those people posting for you. The police will have to look into it now."

"Maybe." Halla didn't look convinced.

"They posted them on his blog first, but he started moderating comments," Saffron said through the speakerphone. "I think the pastor might have started the Go Fund Me account, and maybe he's not online yet to delete them there. But even when he does, they've commented on all the Facebook posts as well, and Halla's dad can't delete comments on other people's pages, so it's going viral. They've also emailed Go Fund Me directly, asking for the payments to be halted. I've made screen shots of everything. We're all posting them."

I looked at Tessa. "What do you think?"

"I think it's a great way to catch a rat."

"He's not going to be happy," Halla said, her voice trembling. "He'll do something."

"But not to you," I said. "He doesn't know where you are. By the time he does, we'll get my friend at DCS to stop him."

"No. Not yet. Please?" Halla looked frightened.

But I knew I had to act—and soon. Jameson had been right all along about getting legitimate. I needed the support, and these girls needed to live without fear. Besides, I felt I now had enough proof and support to free Halla from her father forever.

Even so, I nodded. She didn't need to know what I was going to do. I could spare her the knowledge as I had Ruth until I could work it out. Sometimes being the adult meant doing what was right, especially when it was difficult.

Jameson and I met Bea at the nearly deserted DCS offices on Sunday after church. She was wearing jeans instead of the suit attire she normally used when popping in at Teen Remake. Elsie was holding so tightly to my hand that I'd lost all feeling in my fingers, but I didn't let her go.

I turned her toward me and bent over slightly to look into her eyes. "We're never going to stop fighting. Got that? I don't know what's going to happen, but you hold onto those words. I'm going to fight for you, no matter how long it takes."

Jameson stared down at us, moisture glittering in his eyes. "That's right. Me too. And if we have to, we'll run away to another country."

My jaw dropped. This from my toe-the-line, letter-of-the-law, trust-the-system boyfriend? If I'd still had any reservations about him, they were gone now. I loved him for that comment.

Really loved him.

For a moment, I didn't know what to do with the knowledge. It was wonderful and exciting and mind-shattering all at once, yet it vied with the devastation I felt over having failed Elsie. There should be fireworks and rockets and celebration. We should be in each other's arms.

But we were exactly where we wanted to be: helping Elsie. Together.

He took Elsie's other hand and tapped on the door.

Bea was waiting for us, her desk here utterly clean except for three neat piles of paper. Jameson placed a folder we'd made on top of one of her piles. It contained blown-up copies of the photographs I'd taken the day I'd found Elsie. My notarized statement was accompanied by one from Payden, Zoey, Bianca, Saffron, and Ruth. Halla had been upset that we hadn't let her make one, but if things didn't go well when we told Bea about her situation, we planned to keep her whereabouts a secret.

Elsie was trembling and crying now, so I pulled her onto my lap as we sat, though she was really too big for that.

Bea's eyes were sad as she regarded Elsie. "First off, I'm here unofficially. I can't take Elsie today, or anything like that. Just so you know." Elsie's body slumped against me in relief.

"Elsie," Bea continued, "the reason you're here is that I wanted to ask you about your mom. I've done some research, but I haven't been able to locate her. Do you know where your mother is? Because if we knew, we could get her statement and that would really help us."

Elsie whispered something, and I had to lean down to catch it. "She says her mother left two years ago."

"She left? Are you sure?" Bea looked at us significantly. Did she suspect that something else had happened to Elsie's mother?

"She sent me a birthday card." Elsie looked up to say.

"Are you sure it was from her?"

Elsie nodded and pulled off her backpack. Her hand disappeared inside and out came a ragged envelope I'd never seen before. From it, she removed a card with a bluebird flying near a tree. Inside it read: *Happy birthday, darling. I will always love you.*

I didn't know how that was true, if she'd left Elsie with a man who physically abused her, but the tender way Elsie held the card told me she believed.

"May I see that?" Bea examined the envelope, but I'd

already seen that there was no return address. She gave it back.

As Elsie put it away, she said, "She left because he was going to kill her." She looked at me, and I could see the unasked question there: Why didn't she take me?

I had no answer.

Bea asked what seemed like a million questions, and to my surprise, Elsie answered them. She told us her father hadn't started hitting her until a few months after her mother left. Before, he'd scream and yell, but it had been her mother who'd taken the brunt of the abuse. Finally, Bea got to the question I'd wanted to ask Elsie for a long time.

"Has your father ever touched you in your private places, somewhere that makes you feel uncomfortable?"

Elsie glanced at me, her face even more frightened. "Go ahead, answer her. It's important." I'd suspected since she arrived that Elsie feared her father or someone sexually, because every time anyone mentioned how pretty she looked, she curled in on herself and a darkness would pass over her face.

"He never touched me, but . . ." She swallowed hard. "I think he watched me when I was in the bathroom. I don't know how. He says things that he couldn't know, and he touches my hair. Or sometimes, he'll rub his hand over my back." She looked at me helplessly. "I don't know how to explain, but it's not like when you or Jameson touch me. It's . . . creepy."

I knew exactly what she meant because I'd dated guys like that. It was in their eyes, the comments they made: lust, intent, darkness.

My gaze flew to Bea's, and I saw my worry reflected

there. She asked a few more questions without learning additional information, and then asked Jameson to take Elsie out to the hallway.

When they were gone, she said, "I'm not going to pretend this isn't difficult. Mr. Reynolds contacted our office as well as the local police when he tracked Elsie here, and someone in my office searched our records for any trace of her. Sometimes we get kids who won't tell us their names, or who don't know their names, and they were all examined carefully. Reynolds is playing the bereaved parent, and as far as I can tell, everyone believes him. In fact, the social worker I talked to was completely charmed by the man. I'm really worried."

"What about the abuse?"

"Oh, my gut tells me it occurred. What's more, I think there's a likelihood he will sexually abuse her in the future. However"—she opened the file we'd brought and took out one of my pictures—"this is the only thing we have to substantiate Elsie's claims. And we have no proof that he was the one who did this to her."

"What about Elsie's testimony?"

"Kids lie about their parents all the time. They lie so much they often start to believe the lies." She held up a hand to prevent my objections. "Yes, the pictures prove she's not lying, but at this point, he could contest that it happened after she left his home."

"What about his delay in trying to find her? She's been with me seven and a half weeks now, and she ran away from home at least a week before that. Yet he sent out flyers only three weeks ago, and he told me personally that she'd been gone only two weeks."

"It just boils down to his word against yours. He'll say he was looking, just not in Phoenix. The photos do at least give our agency enough evidence to conduct oversight, and I'll put in an emergency request for an inquiry, but I'm not going to lie to you—I think he'll get her back. Afterward, there'll be a home visit or two, some interviews. Or there will be as long as he doesn't move and drop off our radar. He might be kind to her for a while, but even if he is physically abusive, she probably won't tell on him for fear it will make things worse because she's already been sent back once."

"I can't let her go back to him."

Her voice took on a weariness I had never associated with her. "I know you want to stop this, but if you run with her, you'll be liable for kidnapping, and you'll lose your other foster children."

I shut my eyes to hold back the stinging tears. "Isn't there anything we can do?"

Bea nodded. "We find the mother. Assuming she really did leave on her own."

And that he didn't kill her.

"Her maiden name is Michelle Luce." Bea pushed a sheet across the desk. "You didn't get this from me, but it contains all the information I've been able to gather since last night on the mother's family, including what we have from our contact in the police department. There have been no hits on the mother for two years. Absolutely nothing."

"So she might very well be dead."

Bea inclined her head. "Or in hiding. Her family might be able to give us a clue which."

"What about before the two years? Is there anything else that might help us? Didn't anyone notice Michelle was being abused by her husband?"

"There are several doctor reports over a ten-year period about suspicious broken bones, but nothing was ever proven, and Michelle never verified anything herself. That's all. But abusers learn how to do the most damage without calling attention." Bea's fingers tapped on the desk, as though releasing pent-up energy. "I'm afraid the family is our only lead. Michelle's parents are dead, but she has a sister, an aunt, and five cousins. Like Elsie's father, they're from Tempe, but they've spread out some. Only one of the cousins is out of state. I'll send someone out myself to chat with those who live here, of course, but without proof that Reynolds has done something wrong, he's going to look a lot like a victim himself. You know, wife leaves him with a child and runs off with a lover or something."

"In other words, you think we have more vested in finding her than they would."

"Exactly. And maybe you can get something more out of Elsie that will help."

"So if we find her mother—"

"And if she agrees to make a complaint against her husband," Bea interjected, "then we can put in place a temporary order to keep her in a foster home or with her mother."

"With her mother?" That made me angry. "You mean the woman who abandoned her?"

Bea smiled and interlaced her fingers on the desk. "Lily, when you've been at this as long as I have, you will learn there are many reasons mothers leave, but some of them actually end up making good parents once they straighten out whatever caused them to break down. As much as I can see you're bonding with Elsie, the best thing for her, if her mother is healthy and ready to take on a child, is to be with her mother. But keep in mind it's not a competition. There's room for everyone in Elsie's life. Don't judge Elsie's mother for doing this. Not until you know everything."

I nodded, because Bea did have more experience, and I hadn't mistaken that look of longing in Elsie's eyes. I felt like weeping, but I managed to choke out. "Okay."

Silence fell, and I took that as my cue to get to my feet, but as I did, Bea spoke again. "I did go to see Ruth's mother this morning, with the social worker who was originally assigned to them. My colleague wasn't exactly excited about working on the weekend, but I find that Sunday mornings tell me a lot about a family."

Reaching out to steady myself on the desk, I held my breath against the possibility of bad news. "And?"

"And I can tell you that after what we heard from them both, Ruth is never going back there. Unless she wants to, of course."

The tears I'd held in check spilled over. I'd embrace any good news at this point. "Thank you. I don't know what you did. Wanda seemed so determined."

"She's more determined to stay out of jail. We'll talk more next week, but you're pushing things at your current apartment, if you want to keep Ruth with you. I could send her somewhere else—"

"No! Please. I'll figure it out."

Bea shook her head, looking up at me. "You know, if you can get through all this, you are either going to be the best single foster parent I've ever known, or the biggest pain in the butt. I'm hoping for the former. Don't disappoint me."

I nodded, clutching the paper she'd given me like a lifeline.

"Well," she said when I didn't leave. "Is there something else?"

This was the third time she'd asked me that question, and this time I was going to tell her the truth. "There is one more thing."

She sighed and indicated the chair. "What's her name?"

I sat down again. "Halla."

When I'd told her everything, she tried to look at the Go Fund Me, but the page had vanished. "We have screenshots," I told her, "but it's also all over Facebook, and Jameson—Mario, I mean—contacted the neighbor himself. He can give you the information."

"Have him email it to me. If this evidence is true, there's a good likelihood we can get the father to back off completely." She arched a brow. "*Now* are we done?"

Saffron would be eighteen in a month, and we'd already decided there was no way she wanted to be tossed into the Social Services do-good machine. "Yeah, we're done."

"I'll get to work on all this, then. Let me know if you find out anything about Elsie's mother."

I slowly walked toward the door, where I stopped and turned around. "What happens to kids like Elsie when they're sent back? In the long run, I mean?"

Bea's mouth became a tight line, and then she said, "Depends on how bad it is. Mostly, they endure until they're old enough to leave. If it's really bad, they run again, which at Elsie's age opens her up to a lot of other dangers. Sometimes they die from abuse."

Not very comforting.

In the hallway, Elsie and Jameson were playing something on his phone. Her face was somber, but she was intent on the game, and I motioned for Jameson to join me. As we walked some distance away, I told him what Bea had said about finding Elsie's mother.

We glanced down the hall to see her watching us, her entire body tense. Did she think we were talking about turning her over?

"Let's get her out to the car and see if she knows anything," Jameson said. "We can go visit the most likely relatives today. Maybe call the others." His hand slid up my arm, leaving a trail of warmth.

"Thank you. But you don't have to . . . this isn't really your . . . I . . ." I no longer knew what I was trying to say, and each time I began it sounded like I didn't want him with me.

"We're in this together. You should know that by now." His voice chided me gently, but his eyes emitted that same warmth as his hand, sending much-needed heat into my numb heart.

"I can't fail her."

"We'll do everything we can."

In the car, we told Elsie everything Bea had said. I didn't want to hide any of the facts; she was twelve, not a baby. Old enough to have run away.

"I don't know where my mom went," she said. Tears leaked from her eyes.

"Were she and her sister close?" Jameson asked.

Elsie shrugged. "They talked on the phone sometimes."

"Did anyone come over?"

"Yeah, Felicia. She's my mom's cousin, I think. They used to laugh a lot." A fleeting smile slid across her face. "She was over a lot when I was little. But she didn't like my dad. They had a huge fight, and then she didn't come anymore. Mom was weird after that. She slept a lot. Sometimes she went to a doctor." Pain filled the last words.

I put my arm around her. "Okay, we'll go talk to her. But first we'll drive you back to Tessa's."

"But what if my mom's with Felicia?"

That was exactly what I was afraid of: finding the woman enjoying a wonderful life while her child suffered under the abusive hand of her estranged husband. "She's probably not," I said. "We're just going to see if they know anything. We'll tell you what we learn."

"Promise?"

I nodded. I might soften the truth, but I wouldn't hide it from her.

When we arrived at Tessa's, Elsie turned to me. "Why didn't my mom take me with her?" A gaping chasm of hurt filled those few words.

Bea's admonition not to judge rang in my head. "I don't know. Maybe she didn't have any choice."

15

Felicia Grange lived in Surprise, off Greasewood Street. We decided not to call her but to show up unannounced, hoping we'd learn more.

"We'll surprise her in Surprise." Jameson's joke was lame, but I smiled anyway to show I appreciated the effort. "I've been looking at some apartments here for you," he added. "Haven't found much of anything."

"Bit of a commute to Teen Remake." Forty minutes about—forty long minutes that had me wondering if I'd done the right thing leaving Elsie with Tessa. What if the police came for her while we were gone? Nothing I could do about that now.

Felicia Grange lived in a tan and red two-story apartment in the middle of similar dwellings. The place looked much better than where I lived now but was still compact, perhaps designed for couples with young children or empty nesters who didn't want the burden of a yard.

She was home, which was a stroke of luck for us, but her slightly bulging green eyes narrowed the second we mentioned Michelle. "I don't know where she is," Felicia said, leaning against the edge of her partially open door as if she wanted to slam it on us.

"Please, can we just come in for a moment?" I asked. "We're not just looking for Michelle. It's about her daughter, Elsie."

Felicia's tight mouth softened slightly. "Okay." She pulled the door open and let us in, adjusting her messy ponytail slightly. Her hair was blond, and I wondered if Michelle's was too.

"Please, have a seat." Felicia indicated the brown leather couch. "I'll be back; I'm going to tell my husband I need a few minutes."

She disappeared up the nearby stairs, and I immediately popped up to examine the pictures on the wall. There were some of Felicia with a man, whom I presumed was her husband, and only one of a much younger Felicia with a thin blond woman. The photograph was slightly blurred, and I couldn't really make out the woman's features, but the child in her lap reminded me a lot of Elsie.

"Think that's her?" I asked.

Jameson nodded. "Looks like Elsie in her lap."

Felicia was laughing, but the smile on Michelle's face didn't quite reach her eyes.

"Elsie was four," said Felicia from behind us.

I started at her voice. "Is this her mother?"

"Yeah."

Jameson and I returned to the couch, while Felicia dropped onto the matching loveseat. "I'll get right to the point," I said. "Elsie ran away from her father a couple months ago after he beat her severely, and not for the first time. I found her near a Dumpster in Phoenix, trying to forage for food. She's been with me ever since."

"He beat her?" Felicia shook her head. "Oh, no."

"Yes, and now he's trying to take her home, and DCS pretty much is going to hand her back to him." I hesitated before adding. "I have reason to believe that his abuse is starting to become sexual."

"But you'll fight him from taking her back, right?" Felicia said.

"Of course. But you don't understand. It's her word against his, and everyone believes him."

"Everyone always believes Brad," she said bitterly. "I told Michelle not to marry that jerk. He was controlling and mean. They hadn't been married six months before he began to hit her."

"So she left," I prompted.

"Eventually. It took thirteen years too long, if you ask me."

"Why didn't she take Elsie?" I tried to hold in my anger at the words.

Felicia looked away, her eyes going to the photograph on the wall, though she couldn't possibly see Michelle or Elsie's faces. "She was expecting again, and she lost the baby because he hit her. She ended up in the hospital with all the blood she lost. She started taking prescription meds. I told her she needed help—that they both needed help—but the drugs made her compliant, and she didn't care anymore. It was like she was dying right in front of me. I had it out with Brad, and then suddenly she stopped answering my calls. Or maybe she didn't have a phone any more. I went there at least a dozen times during the day when I knew he wasn't home. No one answered."

"You think she might be dead?" My words sounded too loud in the silence of the room.

"No. Two years ago, she called me from a mall, higher than a kite. Asked me to come get her. She slept for two weeks straight, popping pills whenever she woke—prescription ones—and when those ran out, she found more. I don't know where. I asked about Elsie, but she wouldn't answer." Felicia frowned, her face grim. "If Michelle had stayed with Brad, she'd be dead. I don't doubt it. She wasn't okay. I don't know if she'll ever be okay. She can't be, or she'd never have left Elsie."

I clenched my hands with frustration. "Where is she now? If she could testify to any of this, we could save Elsie."

"Really? She's a drug addict. I don't see how anything she says will help."

"Just tell us where she is."

"I don't know. I hooked her up with a place that helps people with addiction, and she calls every now and then from a payphone, still high a lot of the time. I'm sorry." Felicia seemed sincere, but there was something odd about the way she met my gaze, as if doing so made her uncomfortable.

"I don't see how she can help," Felicia continued, "but if she calls, I can ask her to call you."

"What about you?" Jameson asked. "Would you be willing to testify against him? If you could, maybe that would stall him long enough for us to find Michelle."

"I can, but I never saw him hurt her. I saw bruises,

that's all. No one has ever seen him hit her. He's really careful."

"Well, something set him off." Jameson drew out the new copies he'd made of my photographs. "If we don't do something, this is what's in Elsie's future."

Felicia gasped. "Oh, no. Oh, poor baby."

"Please tell us something," I said. "What about her other relatives? Her sister? Were they close?"

Felicia tore her gaze from the photographs of Elsie. "Michelle's sister lives in Peoria, if you want to ask, but she's a lot older, and they were never close. I doubt she'd contact her. Same with my brother, and our two other cousins. All much older."

"What about your mother?"

"She passed away. We have an aunt, who's in a rest home. She's got dementia, though, and half the time she doesn't recognize her own children."

Felicia had just covered all the other relatives, but that didn't mean I wasn't going to check them out. "Okay," I said, standing abruptly, wanting to get to the next address on the list. "At least when the police and the social workers contact you, tell them the truth."

"They'll be contacting me?" No missing the consternation in her voice. "But I don't know where she is."

"Then I guess that's what you tell them."

Felicia walked with us to the door. "You will find a way to help Elsie. You have to. They can't let her go back to him. He"—she gave a shudder—"always made me feel he was undressing me with his eyes, you know?"

"Unfortunately, we can't stop him. The only thing DCS can do is visit."

"That'll be enough. He won't dare hurt her again."

I turned to her on the step. "Beating or molesting a child isn't the only way to hurt them. Given your experience with Michelle, you should know there are other ways. One of my foster girls has a father who handcuffed her to her bed for weeks. At this point, Elsie's best bet is to run away again, but it won't be to me because I'll be the first place the police will look. All she'll know is that every single adult in her life failed her."

Tears glittered in Felicia's eyes, making them bulge even more. "I'm sorry. I really am."

"You know what's really sad?" I said. "She keeps a card her mother sent her and prays she'll come back. But her mother isn't coming back for her, is she? Not ever."

Felicia opened her mouth and closed it without saying anything. Then she tried again. "Michelle does care, but she's too afraid of him. I think that's why she can't stop the drugs. And drugs change everything."

"I'll tell that to Elsie." I wouldn't of course, but I couldn't stand anyone giving Michelle a break, not when it came at Elsie's expense.

I left Jameson to give Felicia our contact information. She tried to pass back the photographs, but he didn't take them. "In case Michelle shows up," he said, and hurried after me.

In the car, he didn't start the engine right away. "If you tell me not to judge," I muttered, "I swear, I'm going to hit you."

"No. I just wanted to ask which address we're going to next."

We visited Michelle's sister in Peoria, a cousin in Glendale, and two more cousins in Mesa. The two in Mesa hadn't even heard Michelle was missing. We left pictures of Elsie with all of them, hoping the shocking images would prompt some kind of action. They'd all heard rumors that Michelle's husband was abusive, but none of them had tried to help her, presumably because they hadn't any proof.

I cried silently all the way home, and Jameson said nothing. He just held my hand.

"Did you think something was odd about Felicia?" I recovered enough to ask him as we arrived at Tessa's. "She seemed kind of vague, or distracted."

"You mean like she was hiding something? Maybe. I thought it was weird that she wasn't wearing a wedding ring."

"She wasn't?"

"No." He gave me a crooked grin. "Don't tell me you don't check these things."

"I guess I do, but not for women. Why would she lie about a husband?"

He shook his head. "She looked like she'd slept in really late. She probably just never put her ring on. I hear a lot of women don't wear them at night. But I agree there was something weird about her. She really seemed convinced that Michelle wasn't in control of her actions."

I sighed. "She probably isn't."

"What are we going to do?"

"I can't run, not with all the girls."

"No."

"I guess I'll take the girls home. I might be able to hide Elsie on the roof for a few days, if they come for her. I can't do that at Tessa's. Maybe we'll find Michelle by then."

"You could go to jail."

"That's a risk I'm going to have to take."

"Come on." He took my hand, and we went inside.

Our plans changed again when Bea called before we were ready to leave Tessa's to let us know the police had interviewed my neighbors and tracked the address information I'd listed with Teen Remake. "I'm really sorry," she said, "are you there now?"

"Yes."

"Well, they're on their way over. I had to tell them she was with you. Please, just turn her over, and I swear I'll do my best for her." Bea used a falsely bright voice, and I knew it was for my benefit.

"They're coming right now?" I asked.

"Actually, they're probably already there. Or nearly."

My eyes met Elsie's, and she started to shake her head. "No, no," she whispered.

I hung up the phone and hugged her tightly while the other girls peppered me with questions. "Honey, we're going to figure things out," I told Elsie. "Somehow. You're strong. You can get through this." I sank down to the couch, pulling her with me. "I want you to do exactly what he says. No backtalk, nothing."

"He'll still get mad. He even yells at the TV."

How can I possibly let her go?

I couldn't. I was getting her out of there now. "Come on! Let's go, girls. Just leave everything. We'll get it later."

"Lily, no," Tessa said.

"They can't take her if they can't find her."

"You'll go to jail."

"I don't care."

We were halfway across the room when the doorbell rang. Tessa sprinted ahead of us and looked through the peephole. "It's the police. I have to open it."

"I'll talk to them," Jameson said.

Ignoring them, I gripped Elsie's shoulders. "Be strong," I whispered. "I will do everything to get you out of there. I promise." It felt like a lie. Hadn't I already done everything?

Tears streamed down her face. "I know."

"We're looking for Lily Crawford and Elsie Reynolds," I heard an officer say at the door. "Are they here?"

Elsie fumbled in her backpack and pulled out her mother's letter. "Keep this for me. He'll throw it away. I'll get it later."

"Okay." What else could I say? It was her most precious possession, and she was entrusting it to me. "You have my number memorized, right? You need me, you call. Even if you just want to talk. Borrow a phone from the neighbors or anyone you can. Do whatever you need to do."

"I'll try."

"Elsie?" A blond-haired woman with the two officers came toward us. "I need you to come with me, honey. Everything's going to be all right."

I wanted to scream that it wouldn't be all right, but I didn't want to scare Elsie or the other girls.

One by one, the girls hugged Elsie and whispered encouragement. Jameson hugged her too, and his devastated expression resembled my own.

Elsie put her hand in the woman's and looked back as they left. Wearing her pink backpack and with the stuffed wolf I'd bought her clutched to her chest, she looked so young and defenseless. Her eyes grabbed onto my heart and took it with her.

16

"There's got to be something we can do," Ruth said as we sat around our apartment moping the next day. I nodded. "We'll go see her. He can't stop us from visiting."

"My father could," Halla said darkly. "He stopped everyone." She looked as if she hadn't slept at all, which she probably hadn't, worrying she'd be the next one the police came for.

Saffron appeared ready to burst into angry tears. Of all the girls, she hadn't been there to say goodbye, and it bothered her. "We won't take no for an answer."

It was all talk. I knew it, if they didn't. We would try, but ultimately that angry man would control the situation.

"She'll run away again. I know she will," Zoey said. "That's what I would do." The other girls murmured in assent.

"If she can," Halla muttered.

Saffron's chin went up. "Maybe we should help her."

I had to say something to turn things around before they made it worse. "One good thing happened yesterday,"

I said. The girls looked at me hopefully, as I continued, "I went to see Ruth's mom last week, and I found out—" Belatedly, I realized that I should probably be talking to Ruth alone. "Ruth, maybe I should tell you first."

"No, no. Go ahead. What'd she say?"

I chose my words carefully. I didn't want her to feel rejected, but I didn't want her to run back there either. "She has new boyfriend, and in talking to her, it became apparent that while she could use your hand keeping the house tidy, it wouldn't be good for you to live with him."

"He's a creep, isn't he?"

"Yeah, but that's good because now it's official. You can stay with me."

Her mouth dropped. "Really? Why didn't you tell me when you went to see her?"

"I didn't want to get your hopes up."

She hugged me tightly. "I can go to school?"

"Yes. Oh, yes."

Zoey rolled her eyes. "You'll be hating it soon enough." The girls laughed.

"What about finding a new place to live?" Saffron asked. "They won't let you keep three foster kids here, will they?"

Bianca's brow furrowed. "But if we move, Elsie won't know where to find us."

We were back where we began. Was Elsie already with her father? Probably. Was he behaving himself? Had he hit her for leaving? "She has my phone number, so she can call. But Saffron's right that I had better get started on finding a new apartment. Why don't you help me?"

Taking my laptop, I sat on the couch with the girls

crowded around me. I had to go pick up groceries from Payden in an hour, at the very latest. What would I tell him? He'd be as upset as the rest of us.

"I don't like any of these apartments," Ruth said after fifteen minutes of searching. "Not one of them will let us have a dog."

"I guess we'll have to do without a dog for a while," I said.

"Wait, wait, wait!" Saffron looked up from her phone. "Oh, you're not going to believe this." We all stared, eager to hear more. "Halla," Saffron continued, "your dad just sent three of the girls who posted on his blog a private message threatening them. Said he'd blow their heads off and bury them in the woods if they didn't stop posting on Facebook. Is he a total idiot?"

"When he's mad, yes." Halla leaned over to look at Saffron's phone. "Once when I was eight, he told me he'd cut me into little pieces and flush me down the toilet if I ever disobeyed him again. Then he brought in his chainsaw and kept it in the upstairs bathroom. I had nightmares for a year."

"Tell them to forward the messages to you," I said. "I need them."

"Why?" Halla asked.

"Because we're going to send them to the newspapers." And to Bea at DCS.

The excitement of the messages occupied us until even after we went to Payden's store for the expired groceries. I felt guilty at being grateful for the distraction, and a little disloyal to Elsie. But I wasn't giving up. I called Bea four times, and got her answering machine.

Jameson came over, bringing food and videos, but no one was in the mood, and the girls ended up going to sleep early. I didn't blame them.

The strange call came after Jameson left, from a blocked number. "Hello?" I asked.

A breath and then nothing.

"Who is this? Elsie?"

No answer. The line was dead.

Monday crawled into Tuesday and even more slowly into Wednesday. There was no news about Elsie. I called the number Reynolds had listed on his flyer about Elsie, but the number was no longer working. After three more calls to Bea, she finally rang back and told me to stop, that she'd let me know if they had news about Elsie's mother, or if the caseworker discovered something unusual at the home visit scheduled for the first of next week.

I tried to busy myself looking for another part-time job, but the offerings were slim, especially since I'd have to give the job up when I started school again in the fall. If I didn't have a full tuition scholarship, I might not go back at all because I still didn't know what I should graduate in. Besides, with all the girls home, I was busy finding them activities—anything but computer games or television all day. If I had to work another job, I didn't know what they'd do. So far we'd learned how to cook three different dishes, and Makay had taken them grocery shopping with coupons.

I missed Elsie, and worry about her was slowly eating

at my composure. I was sure the blocked call had been from her. Why didn't she call back? Had he caught her calling and forbidden it?

It was almost dinner time when Ruth asked the question on my mind, "Do you think Elsie's okay?"

No, I didn't think she was. I grabbed my purse from the counter. "Look, I'm going out for a drive."

Zoey looked up from the stack of magazines she'd found discarded near our apartment Dumpster. "Where?"

"Can I come?" Ruth asked. "I'm bored."

Saffron tore her gaze from her phone. She was off work and apparently didn't have a date tonight because her boyfriend was working. "I'm in. Where we going?"

"We could get some videos," Halla said hopefully.

"No. I'm going to see Elsie's mother's cousin. Again. She knows something about Elsie's mother—I feel it."

"I'm definitely going," Zoey said, accompanied by a chorus of agreement from the others.

I texted Jameson about my plan, and he shot back, *Almost there. Wait for me?*

Felicia opened the door only about a foot, but she didn't seem surprised to see us again, despite our increased numbers. "These are our foster girls," I said. "May we come in?"

Felicia kept her hold on the door. "I don't think so. I'm about to leave." Her long hair did look freshly styled, but she still wore no wedding ring.

"Have you heard from Michelle?" I asked.

"No. I told you I'd call. Why, did something happen?"

"They gave Elsie back to her father on Sunday night. There's been no word from her. I think she might have called me on Monday, but she hung up before she said anything. Or someone made her hang up."

Felicia's upper teeth worried her lower lip. "I didn't think they'd give her back to him."

"What do you mean?" I was glad Jameson was holding my hand or I might be tempted to smack her. "We told you they would."

"You know where Michelle is," Jameson said, "don't you?"

Felicia let out a long breath. "You don't understand. She's so fragile. This could set her back. She's barely off the drugs, and she's afraid she'll have to go back to him. She can't survive that."

"She's an adult. No one can force her to go back to him. Not like they can Elsie. She has no one to protect her. Michelle doesn't even have to see him. Or Elsie, for that matter. We just need someone to verify Elsie's story. Even if there's no proof, it'll be enough to help. Please. She's just a little girl. I'm not asking Michelle to take care of Elsie or be responsible for her—or for you to take her—I just want her safe."

Felicia started to shake her head, but the door was suddenly pulled from her hands, opening all the way to reveal a painfully thin woman I barely recognized from Felicia's photograph as Michelle. I searched her for signs of similarity to Elsie, but there was none. Michelle had blond hair, a sallow complexion, and her green eyes were far too large in her thin face. Elsie definitely took after her father.

"There is proof," she said. "I have some notes he wrote, pictures of me—what he did. It was to save her when I could. I thought it would only be a few months, but I've been . . . not right in my . . ." She touched her head. "He'd kill me if he could. Maybe he still will."

Felicia grabbed her arm. "He's not going to find you. I know a place you can stay."

"I called him a few months ago," Michelle continued, as if her cousin hadn't spoken. "I asked him if he'd let me see her." She wiped tears as they fell from her eyes. "He said he'd kill us both if I called again. I recorded that too."

"Will you come with us to DCS?" I asked Michelle. "They need to hear this." I didn't mention the police because I was fighting for Elsie, and it might scare Michelle off, but I'd make sure they were there as well.

Michelle nodded, and Felicia said, "We'll both come."

For the second time, Bea Lundberg met us outside of regular hours at the DCS office. With her was a police officer, but to my surprise, Michelle didn't balk. They listened as she told her story, and I breathed a sigh of relief when she turned over a small packet of notes and pictures.

Bea grinned at us. "This is enough for a full inquiry, and to remove Elsie from the home as an emergency measure. I'm sure once the police question him and the psychologists are allowed to talk to Elsie, they'll get what we need. Reynolds wouldn't agree to it before. Now he has no choice."

I stood up. "Great. When can we get her back?"

"Not until tomorrow, I'm afraid. We'll need to get our attorney involved and a signed order by a judge. And a police officer to go with the social worker to pick her up."

Tomorrow? It seemed forever away, especially if Elsie was hurt and desperate.

"You'll let me know?"

Bea nodded and went back to talking with the officer about the evidence.

"Come on," Jameson said. "Let them do their jobs. The girls are still waiting out in the hall."

Before we reached the door, Michelle arose from her chair and touched my sleeve, her eyes glistening with unshed tears. "Please understand. Leaving her was the only way I could leave at all. I always planned to go back for her."

I hadn't lived her life. I didn't know what the drugs and desperation had done to her perception. Was there a point when despair made you think only of yourself? I hoped I'd never know.

"You did a good thing here today," I told her. Better than Halla's mother, or Ruth's and Saffron's. "When you're ready, I know she'll want to see you again." It was true, no matter how I disliked the idea.

The tears welled over and fell unchecked down her face. "Thank you for taking care of her. I hope you will still take care of her until . . . for a while."

"Of course." I blinked back my own tears.

We took the girls home and put in a video, but I couldn't watch it. Instead, I paced the small kitchen until Jameson put his arms around me. "I can't stand this," I whispered.

"Then let's go see her. It's barely eight, and I have his address."

"Really?"

"At least you'll be able to tell her it's going to be okay."

Outside the sun had set, but its light still sent red and gold cascading through the clouds across the horizon. It was beautiful, but it was painful too, as I recalled the times Elsie and I had watched a similar sky from the rooftop.

Twenty minutes to Tempe and then I'd know she was okay. "Man, does this get worse with your own kids?" I mumbled. "Because this is awful. Maybe I shouldn't have kids."

"No, because our kids are never going to have to worry about their parents hurting them."

"Our kids?" I asked, my heart doing a little skip in my chest.

"Yeah, yours and mine . . . uh, not necessarily together . . . uh, I just meant . . ." Was he blushing? It was hard to tell with the red reflection of the sky. But I let his comments pass. Now was not the time for a discussion about our future.

The closer we got to Tempe, the more worried I was. "What if he won't let us see her? We can't say anything about Michelle. It might set him off."

Jameson glanced over at me, worried. "You think he might wig out anyway?"

"Maybe." I flopped my head back on the seat. "Oh, this is a bad idea. But I still feel we should go."

"Me too."

There it was. We were admitting it now. It was a feeling, a dread I'd experienced even before I'd decided to go to Felicia's.

The Reynolds lived in an ordinary single-floor house with red stucco, desert landscaping, and a tiny bush near the house. No flowers or anything that hinted of femininity. The ordinariness of the house took me by surprise. How could it not stand out in some way? It should be sinister or unkempt, or at the very least have a *No Trespassing* sign.

"Well?" Jameson asked.

Lights glowed from the main areas of the house, but none came from the other room facing the front. "She's probably in bed."

"At eight-thirty in the summer?"

"Let's go ask." We walked up the steps, moving faster now that we'd actually made the decision. I knocked on the door. Footsteps echoed inside the house and seemed to take forever to reach the door. Then suddenly it opened, and there was Mr. Reynolds, with his dark curling hair and those liquid eyes that most women would drool over.

"Can I help you?" he began. "Wait, I know you. You're that woman who lied about having my daughter."

"That was a mix-up," I insisted. "You said she'd been gone two weeks, and Elsie had been with me for seven and a half. Please, could I just see her for a few minutes? I brought some things she left at my apartment." That had been Jameson's idea. Basically, we'd thrown a couple of candy bars, knickknacks, and a shirt into a bag to pretend to give to her.

"No." Reynolds started to shut the door.

"Please, I just want to give her a hug."

"I said no." His flushed face indicated that he was getting angry.

"Then you give it to her." I thrust the bag at him. At least she'd know I'd been here.

He opened the bag, glanced inside, and tossed it back to me. "Junk. She doesn't need it. Now get off my property." He punctuated his demand with a curse.

As he'd tossed the bag, I'd caught sight of a couple of taped moving boxes in the house behind him, with more folded boxes next to them. Was he going someplace? Bea had mentioned that the one way he might slip away from DCS supervision was to move.

Oh, no. Would Bea's judge give us what we needed before he disappeared? "Please," I begged. "Just for a moment."

Another string of curses. "For the last time, she can't see you. She's asleep."

I glanced at Jameson, feeling a sense of déjà vu. "At eight-thirty?" Something really wasn't right here. You'd think if he was trying to get DCS off his case, he'd be willing to let us talk to her for a few seconds.

Unless he'd hurt her.

Jameson had apparently come to the same conclusion. Or maybe he'd also seen the boxes. "We're not leaving until we see her," he said. "Call the police if you want. We need to make sure she's okay."

Mr. Reynolds eyes widened. "She's *my* daughter." Spittle flew from his mouth with the force of the words. "You have no rights here. Now leave or I'll make you leave." When we didn't move, he threw open his door and dived at us.

Jameson jumped in front of me, hands up to block. Reynolds's fists pummeled into him, catching him in the stomach and face. Jameson stumbled down the two steps and fell into the grass. Reynolds pounced on him. I heard a scream, and I glanced toward the house before I realized it was my own.

More punches as I stood there, frozen with fear. *Move!* I told myself.

Then I was free, pushing my feet down the porch stairs toward them, raising the bag in my hand. The knickknacks might stop him for a moment. But with a grunt, Jameson bucked Reynolds off, blocking and punching back. The two rolled over the cement and into the rock flowerbed until finally Jameson pinned Reynolds under him.

"Go find her," Jameson told me.

"She's not here!" Reynolds spat at him in triumph.

Horror spread through me. "What did you do?"

"Me?" He gave a sharp laugh. "Nothing. That ungrateful brat stole my phone on Monday and took off, but I canceled the service yesterday morning. When I get my hands on her, I'll teach her a lesson."

Not believing him, I shouted into the house, and then finally went inside, calling her name. Moving boxes were everywhere, most of them already sealed. He'd been at this a lot longer than a few days.

I found a child's room, where the bed was neatly made

and all the clothes still in the closet. No Elsie. *No backpack or stuffed wolf, either,* I thought. Reynolds might be telling the truth. To make sure, I checked in all the other closets and unsealed more than a few of his packing boxes.

"I'll sue you for trespassing!" Reynolds shouted when I emerged from the house. His voice definitely carried to the two neighbors heading in our direction.

"She's not here," I told Jameson.

Jameson jumped up from Reynolds as the neighbors arrived. "What's going on here?" asked a big guy who looked like a football player. "You okay?" he added—to Jameson, not Reynolds.

Reynolds climbed to his feet, wiping the blood from his lip. "He assaulted me!"

Jameson held up his hands and backed away. "It wasn't like that."

"We just wanted to talk to his daughter," I added, "and give her the stuff she left at my house." I lifted the bag to show them. "She's been staying with me. Then he went crazy."

The shorter man snorted. "That, I believe."

"Shut your stupid mouth!" Reynolds said with a sneer. He lunged at the short neighbor, but the football player held out his arm to prevent him from landing a punch.

Reynolds wasn't loved by his neighbors, apparently.

"You'd better go," said the shorter neighbor. "I'm sure it was all a misunderstanding like you say. Brad is the king of misunderstanding."

Jameson and I didn't need a second invitation, but I had to ask, "Have you two seen his daughter?" They shook their heads. We hurried back to Jameson's car. He was limping slightly and his eye was darkening, but nothing appeared broken.

"Want me to drive?"

"And wound my manhood? No." He opened the door for me and went around to the driver's side.

"So where is she then?" I asked.

"No idea. But that call you received on Monday was probably her. Something must have happened right then, or the phone lost service, if Reynolds is telling the truth about when he disconnected it. If she left on her own, is there any place she'd go?"

I started to shake my head, but suddenly I did know. "Yes! The park where we found Zoey and Bianca. That's our meeting place if anything goes wrong. Elsie wouldn't go back to the apartment because he'd find her, but she might go there."

"That's twenty minutes by car."

"Elsie's resourceful, and she had his phone, right? It worked for a time."

"She's had two days to get there." Jameson pushed on the gas. "I bet she made it. If she hasn't, we need to call the police."

Jameson might have broken a few speed limits getting us back to Phoenix. Even so, night had fallen completely by the time we arrived at the park. I couldn't get out of the Mustang fast enough, forgetting about Jameson's ruined eye and his hurt leg.

"Elsie!" I shouted when I was still too far away to see if anyone was near our bench. But before I reached it, there she was, coming from another direction, carrying a stuffed backpack and two other large shoulder bags. She dropped them all as she ran to meet me.

"Finally!" she said.

"Sorry it took me so long." I hugged her tightly, and she winced. "Are you hurt?"

She nodded and drew up her shirt in the back. Even with only the dim illumination from the nearby streetlight I could see the deep bruising.

"I couldn't stay," she said. "After he did it, he said we were going to move, that the social workers would never leave us alone, so we had to get away. I knew if I didn't run, it would be too late."

I hugged her again, more gently. "It's all over. We found a way. You're not going back there again."

"I knew you would. I just didn't know if you could do it in time."

"You did great."

She buried her face in my chest and held on while I smoothed her hair that was once again back to its wild state. Soon I would have to tell her about her mother, but not now. This moment was for us.

Jameson finally caught up to us, and Elsie looked at him, puzzled. "What happened to you?"

"I'll tell you later."

But she wasn't letting it go. "Did my father do that? Did you go see him?"

"Yeah, but I'm okay and so is he."

"I hope you hit him hard."

Jameson grinned. "I did. Come on. Let's get you home."

Back at our apartment, while the girls surrounded

Elsie, we called Bea, and she came with a police officer to take down our statements and get pictures of Elsie's bruises. Elsie waited until they were present to fill us all in about how she'd made it to the park.

"That first night I barely made it close to Phoenix," she said, snuggling against me on the couch. "That was when I gave up and called you. But I'd used all the battery with the GPS, and it died. So I slept in someone's backyard—I brought a blanket this time. I woke up really late the next day, and I got a little mixed up without the map on the phone, so I didn't get to the park until late last night. But I eventually found it." Pride seeped into her voice. "Then I waited there. I was going to borrow someone else's phone to call you, but I had food, and I decided it wasn't too bad living there for a while. I thought it might give you time to find my mom."

I leaned my head against hers. "You should have come home." I couldn't believe she'd been so close all this time. "Something might have happened to you."

"I didn't come back here because I knew that's the first place he'd go."

"But he didn't," Saffron said. "And he probably wouldn't while you have those bruises."

Anger ran through me just thinking about him touching her. "Anyway, I'd have never let him take you after hurting you again."

Elsie looked down at her hands. "Yeah, but I didn't want him to hit you. I was just going to ask if you'd help me get away until you found my mom."

"Ah, honey," Jameson said. "We're not afraid of him. He punches like a girl." That made the girls laugh.

"Well, you still got a black eye," Saffron pointed out.

Jameson shrugged. "Even girls get lucky."

"You ain't going nowhere but with us," Ruth said to Elsie. "We already found your mom, and she's going to testify."

"My mom?" Elsie's expression changed, becoming hopeful and wary.

I took her hand. "She's been wanting to see you, but you'll still stay with us for a while, okay?" I glanced at Bea, who nodded.

"That's right," Bea said. "Your mom's been through a lot. For now, she'll come and visit you while you're with Lily."

Elsie squeezed my hand, looking relieved. "I'd like that."

I was her stability, not her mother. At least not yet, but I needed to accept that my job was helping her and Michelle to a point where Michelle could be a mother again and Elsie could trust her.

After the police officer left, Bea folded her arms and shook her head as she looked around the apartment. "This is never going to pass for all these girls—I can't even give you a temporary pass. The best I can do will be to delay the paperwork until you have something more adequate."

"Actually, I think I might have found a place," Jameson said. "With all that's happened, I didn't even get a chance to tell Lily yet." His voice held suppressed excitement that made me look at him closely.

"Good," Bea said. "June's almost over, so Lily should be receiving the check for Zoey and Bianca any day now for that month, but checks for Ruth, Halla, and Elsie will be a lot longer in coming. I could apply for an emergency payment, though. I'll look into it."

"Did you say Halla?" Halla asked. In all the confusion, she hadn't hidden from Bea or the officer, but she did have her wig on.

Bea turned, her sharp eyes searching Halla's face. "Yes, I said Halla. I know about you, and I'm working on your case now. It's going to take a few weeks to settle this, but for now, you're officially staying here. Or rather, wherever you guys move."

"Yes!" Halla squealed and jumped, raising her fist in triumph. "Thank you!" She pulled off the wig. "Because this thing is horribly uncomfortable."

Everyone laughed, but Bea wasn't finished. Her gazed settled on Saffron. "What I don't know is who are you?"

Saffron raised her hands. "Don't mix me up in this. I'm not a kid. I'm an adult with a job. I just help Lily."

Bea's gaze went to me, and I nodded. "I already told you Saffron was living with me when we first talked about Zoey and Bianca, remember?"

"Right, the one who's almost eighteen. I vaguely remember something about that. It's just as well, because you're only cleared for three foster kids for the first two years, and you've already got too many. Only after two years are you allowed to have five."

"What?" Jameson and I said at the same time. How could we have missed something like that?

Bea raised her hand to silence further protests. "It's not something that usually comes up in the beginning because we never place more than a few children at first. But I realize this is an unusual situation, and like always, we are extremely short on foster parents. I'm going to see what I can do." She sighed. "That seems to be my mantra where you're concerned."

"Uh, thank you?" I said.

Bea gave me a smirk. "I'll be going now. Let me know about the new place."

Ruth walked with her to the door, chattering about their similar hair styles.

Jameson sat down next to me on the couch, the bag of ice I'd given him for his eye leaking over his jeans. "I thought I'd make an appointment for us to see the place I found tomorrow after I get off work. Can you make it?"

I smiled. "Yeah. Thank you."

His hand closed over mine. "Lily, I can honestly say that the past weeks I've known you have been the strangest and most interesting in my entire life."

I wrinkled my nose. "Interesting good? Or interesting bad?" Seriously, I was surprised he hadn't run for the hills to get away from my crazy life.

He moved closer until our faces were only a few inches apart. "Definitely good."

Then he kissed me, and I kissed him back, even with all the girls watching us.

17

J ameson picked me up after work the next day. He was no longer limping, but his eye and the skin around it was mottled black. "How's your eye?" I asked. "Looks painful."

"Lots better. Looks worse than it feels. Ankle's good too. Amazing what a little ice and an elastic wrap can do."

We talked on the drive, but his comments were distracted. I'd never seen him so nervous. "It's okay," I told him. "If I don't like it, we'll just find something else. Bea will give us a few more days."

"You'll like it. But, well, it's not perfect." Then he hurried to add, "But it could be with some work."

Work? What kind of an apartment took work? And why was it so far away from downtown?

I had my answers when he pulled into a residential area with older houses set far apart. He stopped the Mustang in front of a white two-story Victorian with a covered wraparound porch. It was big and the lines were beautiful, but it was, kindly put, a horrible wreck. The paint was peeling, the porch railings were missing or broken, the glass in almost every window was busted and patched with cardboard and duct tape, the screen on the front door was ripped, part of the rain gutter hung loose, and the overgrown yard looked like something from a horror movie.

To me it might just be The House.

"How many bedrooms?" I asked, climbing from the car without taking my eyes from the house.

"Seven, and there's enough land out back to extend the house, if it's ever needed. The fields on either side and out back don't belong to the house, but the owners might be persuaded to sell them in the future. I think the yard's plenty big as it is."

"Can we go inside?"

"Yeah. The neighbors down the way have the key, and they should have unlocked the door for us. They're related somehow to the owner."

We passed a picket fence that was more gray than white and had at least a dozen fallen or damaged boards. The walkway was also cracked and broken and would need replacement.

"About the only thing that doesn't need fixing is the roof," Jameson said. "That's why it's still integrally sound. But I'm afraid the inside is just as bad as out here."

"You saw it before?"

"Yesterday on my lunch break. I wanted to make sure there was a possibility before I brought you here. Actually, my dad came to look at it as well. He knows about these things."

Antonio had come to look at my house? The idea made me feel almost weepy.

Jameson hadn't exaggerated about the inside. Every single bit of carpet would need replacing and all the walls repainting. Many would have to be repaired first. There were four bathrooms, but they were all missing toilets. The master bedroom was on the main floor, looking over the back yard and the fenced field beyond. It had a private bathroom and a little alcove for a desk or maybe a crib.

The rest of the rooms were small, but enough for two beds. There was a mudroom, and I could envision a row of wooden lockers for each of the girls.

The kitchen was the biggest mess of all, but it was spacious. Plenty of room for a large table, though the tiny window in the dining area would need to be replaced with something five times that size. Was that even possible? It had to be. The yellow laminated countertops weren't beautiful, but they were in decent shape. Even the cracked linoleum might be salvaged for a time, though it would be the first to go if I found the money.

I'd have to find used appliances to replace those that were missing, and the cupboards needed sanding and painting. *White,* I thought. It would be so much nicer and more welcoming than that scuffed, dark color.

It was definitely The House. My house.

I turned to Jameson, who was looking at me with a hesitant expression in his eyes. "It's perfect," I said, taking both his hands. "Absolutely perfect."

He threw back his head and laughed. "Only you could see the potential in this mess."

"But you worried I wouldn't."

"Kind of. You didn't grow up like this; I did, and I know it can work."

I hugged him, kissing him firmly on the mouth. "Thank you. We can do the work ourselves, if the monthly payments are . . ." I looked down feeling suddenly shy. He'd found the house, but did that mean he was in for the work? Did that mean he wanted me? "The monthly payment . . . it might be more than I can swing."

Jameson blew out a breath that I sensed had worry in it. "Well, the house isn't cheap even in this condition, mostly because of the size and the land, but there are loans that have a balloon payment."

"A balloon payment . . ." My thoughts churned, bringing up what I'd learned about those in my accounting classes. "That's where you pay a lower amount for five or seven years every month, and then you have to pay the rest in one chunk or refinance."

"Exactly. We take the lower monthly payments in the hopes that things will get better in five years." He hesitated several heartbeats before adding, "And they will. We'll both be graduated by then."

We, he'd said. No mistaking that.

My mind was already running along those same lines. In eight years I'd receive my grandfather's inheritance. Eight years, that is, if I was single. If I was married, it would only be three. Three years—which meant in plenty of time to pay down the mortgage enough to refinance, if not pay it off altogether.

We could definitely do it! Of course, Jameson didn't know about my inheritance, or not the details, though I might have mentioned something in passing. It hadn't been relevant until now.

Jameson's hand tightened on mine. "Renting out a

room or two might also be an option, but with my job and yours and some of the foster care money, I think we could—"

"You have to marry me," I said.

Jameson's eyes had a deer-caught-in-the-headlights expression. Did that mean he was averse to the idea? "It's just that I have an inheritance," I hurried on. "I get it when I turn twenty-five, if I'm married. Otherwise, it's not until I'm thirty, and so if we got married, we'd have enough money to—"

He put his hand over my lips. "Really? You're proposing to me? Because of an inheritance? You're ruining everything!" His tone was only half teasing.

I laughed, my confidence surging at his expression. His worry was gone and so was his hesitance. "Yeah, I guess I am. The question is, are you man enough to handle it?"

"Look, maybe you should just zip it for a minute, okay? Let me get a word in edgewise. Because I am *so* not marrying you for an inheritance."

"Okay," I said meekly, but I couldn't help nibbling the finger he still held near my lips.

Stifling laughter, he knelt down on the dusty linoleum and pulled a folded manila envelope from his pocket. A piece of loose tile shifted under his knee, but he simply moved over and started talking.

"You've turned my life upside down since the first day I met you, but I've loved every crazy minute. You're a light to me, and I've seen enough to know that the only way I'm ever going to be happy is if I'm a part of your life. A part of you. I want to slay your dragons, fend off the abusive fathers of our foster girls—or whatever else you need. I want to hold you every night when I go to sleep and see your face first thing in the morning. I want to make love to you knowing that we're never going to end. I love you, Lily Crawford. So much." He opened the flap of the manila envelope. "These are the offer papers I want to put in for the house. I know it's not a ring, but—"

I grabbed the envelope. "It's a thousand times better."

"Will you marry me?"

"I think we already established that." I pulled him up to kiss him, my mouth opening to his. Heat shuddered through me as his tongue slid over mine, setting my skin on fire. I loved this man. I loved his eyes, his mouth, his hands and the way they touched me. I loved his kindness, how good he was with the girls, how willing to step into danger. I even loved his family, and I wanted to spend every second of the rest of my life with him.

"But," I told him, when we came up for breath, "I still asked you first."

He grinned. "That's not the way I remember it. Guess it's your word against mine. But since we're getting married, and I'm already licensed as a foster parent—"

"Wait, you are?"

"Yeah, for two years now, but it's just for emergencies. My roommates don't like it since I have to give up my room and sleep on the couch for however long Bea needs me. But the point is, we can keep all the girls without Bea going crazy."

"Two years? You can have five kids then. That means we can get more."

Jameson laughed. "Can we get moved in first? The

ones we already have are going to make a honeymoon awfully hard."

He kissed me again, and for a long time we forgot about foster girls and houses—and we were almost locked inside the house when the family down the road came to check the doors.

"There is one thing," I said as we walked out to the car, hand in hand. "I'll need to tell my parents."

"I thought we could elope." He winked to show he was kidding.

"That actually might be best."

My parents had big dreams for me, and those didn't include marrying into a blue-collar family and buying a rundown house. I didn't fool myself into thinking they'd come around any time soon. My mother still hadn't talked to me since I refused to go home, except through Tessa when she wanted to make sure I still planned to come home on the Fourth.

That was it. The Fourth was on Saturday, only a few days away, and I could tell them then. If all went well, Jameson could come down on Sunday. Whatever happened, I vowed to make this my last holiday away from the girls. From now on, if my parents wanted me there, it was all of us or nothing. "What are you doing on Sunday?" I asked.

His kisses trailed up my neck to my lips, as if he couldn't get enough of me. "Going to see your parents?"

"Hopefully. You mentioned slaying dragons? Better bring your sword."

18

We gathered the girls and told them the good news—that we were about to spend all the rest of their summer vacation painting, repairing, and otherwise refurbishing an old house. No one seemed to mind.

"I just want to know one thing," Saffron said. "Can I have my own room?" When we nodded, she grinned. "Then I'm in, but I'm paying something for food and rent. I want to pull my weight."

"I think we'll allow that," Jameson said, settling on one of the folded-up chair beds, "just as long as we agree that only married people get to make out in that house. In other words, no boy sleepovers."

"Ah, you take all the fun out of it." Saffron rolled her eyes. "If I ever find a boy worthy of sleeping over, I'd probably marry him. But don't hold your breath because I'm sure he doesn't exist."

The girls began talking about rooms and how they'd contribute to the new house, and the din grew to a point that I almost missed the doorbell. Ruth beat me to the peephole. For a moment I tensed, though I knew Elsie's father had been arrested.

"It's Makay and Nate!" Ruth flung open the door.

Makay was carrying a sleeping Nate and a large suitcase. Her face was white and tear-stained as she struggled under the weight. I took the toddler from her while Ruth grabbed the suitcase.

"What happened?" I asked.

"It's Fern. She died. This is some stuff from her apartment."

"Your stepmother's dead? What happened?"

"It's been so awful."

The girls jumped up from the couch, clearing a place for Makay, which she sank into with a sigh. "I found out this morning," she said. "Apparently, she's been gone a few days." Her face dropped to her hands, as if covering it would remove the image from her mind.

"You found her?" Jameson asked.

Makay lifted her head. "Yes. I called the police. They suspect a drug overdose."

"Why didn't you call me?" I asked, sitting next to her.

"I was fine. It's not like we got along, and all she does is confuse Nate. It was only after we got to the police station that things got bad." She stopped talking, biting her lip to stop herself from crying. "Now I have to prove I'm a fit parent for my brother, or they'll send him to foster care. There's no way they'll ever approve me where I live now. At least I don't think so. I'm pretty sure all my roommates are doing drugs."

"There's a lot more leeway with related siblings," Jameson said. "I'm sure they'll give you time to work it out, but even if they don't . . ." He paused, looking at me. I knew what he was thinking, and it made me love him all the more.

"But I'm only eighteen—well, nineteen in another month," Makay rushed on, missing the look between us. "And I have no family and no real job and no one to leave him with so I can work." She reached to take Nate from me, as if needing him back in her arms. "The social worker who came to the police station told me he'd be better off with an established couple."

I settled him in her arms. "You're Nate's mother—you're all he knows. He belongs with you. But what do you mean, you don't have family? You have us."

"That's right," Halla said. "I'll watch Nate. I've been wishing you'd leave him more. We all have." The other girls murmured in agreement.

Jameson lifted a finger. "Uh, I also know how to babysit. And our new house is going to be plenty big for you and Nate."

Makay looked around us, her panic fading. Suddenly she laughed. "Okay, okay. I'm an idiot, a total idiot. Of course Nate is better off with me, and of course I have all of you. But *our* new house? What did I miss?"

"They're getting married!" Ruth said.

"And buying a big house," Elsie added.

Saffron dropped to the carpet by our feet. "I hope you know how to paint."

"Nope." Makay shook her head. "Not at all. But Google knows everything."

"You mean Bing." Saffron began to type on her phone. "I like that search engine better."

"Whatever. I'm sure we can figure it out." To me, Makay added, "It won't be for long. Just until the adoption is final and I figure things out. Of course, I'll help with rent."

I grinned. "One thing for sure is that wherever you live, you'll always have plenty of babysitters."

Jameson pointed at himself and mouthed. "I'm the best."

Once again a holiday had rolled around, bringing me another girl, this time Makay, a little older than the others, but every bit as much mine. The other two additions, Nate and Jameson, made it the best holiday yet.

My mother finally called me on Friday. Because of the holiday, there was no Teen Nature campout, and I'd spent the day with Jameson and the girls picking out paint colors. I'd decided to let them each decorate their rooms however they wanted, except for the carpet, which I'd choose. Paint was changeable, but not carpet.

"Hi, Mom," I said. Could she tell anything was different by the tone of my voice? The entire world felt different to me now with my future looking so bright.

"I'm just calling to make sure you really are coming."

"Yes, Mom." I walked away from Jameson and the girls so they wouldn't hear. "Hey, I was wondering how you'd feel if I brought some of my friends."

"Friends?" Her voice was wary. "Do you mean those girls? Sweetheart, I know you're helping them, but surely you can spend just one day alone with your parents. Just one."

She really knew how to lay on the guilt. It wasn't so much the words, but the wounded, put-upon tone. Fine. I'd give her this one final day. "Okay, Mom."

"Good." She was all peaches and cream now, the kind of cream that was sour just under the surface.

I hung up and stared into the rows of paint cans, seeing nothing, my happy mood shattered. Then Jameson's hand slid over my back. "Bad news?"

"Just my mom."

He put his arms around me and pulled me close. "You're really worried about tomorrow."

"Yeah. My family . . . they're not like yours."

"So you keep saying, but it's okay. I love you no matter what happens. Are you sure you don't want me to come with you tomorrow? Because I'm willing to talk to them. It doesn't matter what they say about me. Or to me."

"It matters to me."

"I can take it."

"I hope so, because you'll have to on Sunday, and I have the feeling this is a train wreck about to happen."

His laugh filled me with sunlight again. "Good thing we're survivors."

Tessa picked me up early on the Fourth. I felt grouchy at leaving the sleeping girls. They'd be going to a parade later in Arcadia with Jameson, and I'd much rather stay with them. I'd almost canceled the trip to Flagstaff, but I needed to tell my parents about Jameson before he came to meet them tomorrow. Knowing how nervous I was, he'd asked three more times to come with me today, but I wanted to make sure it was okay first. I didn't want his perception of them to be forever colored by their surprise.

"So you're really going to tell Mom and Dad about Mario?" Tessa glanced over at me.

"Yeah. He's a great guy."

"You know they're not going to be happy, right?"

"I know. He's lacking a couple million dollars and a different last name."

"They're not that bad."

I stared at her. I wanted to say, *Yes, Tessa, they are,* but instead I said, "I hope you're right."

"Well, I do really like him."

I grinned. "So do I."

"A big wedding would really help you furnish the house." This time Tessa kept her eyes on the road. If my parents agreed to give me a wedding, she meant. "Are you really going to be able to afford the house?"

"Jameson has a good employment history, and he's been full time for the past two years. I have my record with our company, and Teen Remake gave me a letter saying they plan to keep me on. With my inheritance coming, we've been told we'll be able to get the loan. Coming up with the down payment is the problem."

"Right. A house that size, you have to put down at least ten thousand, right?"

"Actually, they wanted fifteen or twenty, but because of Grandpa's money, they'll take ten."

"And you have that?"

"Not quite. Jameson has been working for two years to save money for college, and he thinks he can put five thousand of that down on the house. Makay talked to this guy she works for, and she says she can get a thousand, which we'll just take off the rent she's going to pay us until we pay her back."

"You don't have any saved?"

"I did, but I spent most of it on the girls. They've needed so much this past year. I think I've got enough left for paint and material for curtains—if Google can teach us how to make them—and I'm planning on using the check I get for the girls to buy used appliances, or at least a fridge and a stove. We've already got mattresses that will have to do for beds. Well, except for Jameson and me."

"You two can use the double mattress and get Zoey and Bianca more of those chair beds."

"Yeah, that'll work. The carpet is the biggest cost, and the windows." I sighed. "Jameson says if we can't get them to go lower on the down payment, he'll work full time another semester or two and use all his savings on the house. He'll probably have to anyway." I made a face. "I'm sad for him to delay it again. I told him I should be the one to work full time, but he doesn't want me to risk my scholarship."

Silence fell as Tessa sped up around a curve. My sister might toe the line with my parents, but she was a bit of a speed demon on the road. "I have money saved," she said. "Close to seven thousand. You can have all of it."

"You can't do that. You might need it."

She flashed me a bored look. "I'm not getting married any time soon, or buying a house. Besides, it's not like you won't have the money to pay me back once you get the money Grandpa left us."

I reached out and took her hand. "Thank you. How about we use just what we need for the rest of the down payment?"

"Okay, but it's there if you need it. I know you, and it's not like you're only going to help girls who are in the foster care system. Like Makay and Saffron. I'm sure there will be others."

She was probably right. I wasn't going to turn any needy girls aside, not as long as I had room to keep them—and now I'd have a lot more rooms to fill.

The two hours under the sweltering sun with my parents at the parade weren't so bad, but the picnic in the park afterward was already shaping up to be something of a horror story. They'd invited the Boswells, whose son, Steve, I'd briefly dated. My mother loved Steve, but his roaming hands and eyes had made our relationship short. Did my mother know me so little that she expected me to lay eyes on the boy and decide I'd been too hasty?

Unfortunately, I knew my mother well enough to know that was exactly what she planned. I groaned. "This is to punish me for having Jameson in my apartment when she came. I just know it."

Tessa giggled. "Man, every time you say Jameson, it throws me off. Should I call him that instead of Mario?"

"Nope." I liked reserving it for myself. Well, and for his mother.

Tessa and I had driven her car instead of riding with our parents, and we'd stopped at a gas station for a cold drink with plenty of ice, which had made us fifteen minutes late to the park.

"Maybe we should just leave," I said, glaring at the Boswells. Sweat dribbled down my back, despite the air conditioning we'd had running in the car.

"Yeah, right." Tessa rolled her eyes. "That would get you off to a good start with Mom and Dad about your new boyfriend."

Fiancé, I wanted to say, but Tessa knew that, and we were too close to the table to discuss it now. Telling my parents about Jameson in front of the Boswells was not an option.

Mother's face flushed as she saw us coming. "There you are. I was beginning to worry. Look who's here, Lily. It's Steve."

"Hi," I said.

Steve grinned. "Hi. Good to see you. I've been meaning to call." He patted the bench next to him.

Great. I sat as far away from him as possible, but he scooted over to close the gap.

The food came out: fried chicken, coleslaw, potato salad, green salad, gelatin, croissants instead of biscuits, chocolate cake, and more. All from a restaurant, of course. I filled my plate with chicken and three flakey croissants.

Steve's hand snaked up my back as he leaned over to say. "Hey, you want to go see the fireworks tonight?" He wasn't bad looking, with dark hair, a nice—if unremarkable—face, and bedroom eyes, but for some reason I couldn't explain, his touch made me cringe.

"Sorry, I can't. Tessa and I have plans."

"That's okay. She can come."

"You kids go ahead," my mother said. "We're staying in this year and watching them from the balcony."

Steve smirked at me, and I shrugged off his hand. "Actually, we're staying in with you guys. I have some things to discuss, and I'm only here for today."

My mother looked ready to argue, and my father's face grew red. They must suspect something. "We'll talk about this later," my father said. "Let's eat."

Not even Steve Boswell dared to go against my father, so everyone fell to eating. I concentrated on the yummy croissants. They weren't quite as good as the ones Jameson had brought to my house, but they were close.

Lunch couldn't end fast enough for me. I finally finished the rest of my three croissants while standing up near Tessa to get away from Steve and his hands. I was anxious to get home, but my parents decided to walk around the park and look at the Fourth of July booths with the Boswells.

"Could you kids pack all this in the car?" my mother asked. "I'm sure Steve will help."

"Love to," he said with a winning smile that made me want to gag.

Mother took me aside. "We'll meet you back at the house. But give him a chance, Lily. He comes from a good family." Not giving me an opportunity to respond, she headed off with my father.

"So, about tonight," Steve began.

"Sorry," I said. "I'm engaged. I just haven't told my parents yet."

He let out a long sigh. "Man, what a wasted afternoon."

"You should have known that already," Tessa told him. "But you can leave now."

"Yeah, right. See you around." He stood and ambled away.

Tessa shivered. "Man, I dislike that guy."

"You didn't have him rubbing your back through half of lunch. Come on, let's get this stuff into their car and go back to the house."

"Why the hurry?"

I smiled sadly. "I want to get as much of my stuff as I can into your car before they come home."

We packed Tessa's car and gathered a bunch of other things to put in Jameson's Mustang when he came tomorrow. I hadn't much use for my belongings at college, but I'd need them as I furnished a new home. Pictures, electronics, knickknacks, bedding—all of it would be useful. My clothing I'd already moved over the past months, but there was a lot I'd left here because I didn't have the room.

Tessa went into our six-car garage and came out with a box of outgrown clothing, old sets of dishes, and small appliances my mother had replaced.

"I already have a toaster," I said.

"You'll need another one." Tessa tucked it in. "Any material or curtains?"

"Not yet. She has a lot of junk out there, though. Might take me weeks to find anything useful."

Tessa's foraging was put to an abrupt halt by our parents' arrival. "Come help me put the leftovers away, girls," Mother said, as our father set the cooler on the kitchen counter. We dug obediently into the cooler, but our mother didn't move to join us. She paused before the large window overlooking our back yard and the horse pasture where Tessa's horse, Serenity, grazed peacefully.

"What's wrong, Mom?" I asked, hoping she didn't have some plan that involved getting rid of the horse. If she did, she'd regret it, because Serenity was the main reason Tessa came home so often.

"Mrs. Boswell heard that an ex-con is buying one of those homes," she said with a disgusted snort, frowning at the tract homes you could barely see through the row of fast-growing trees she'd planted when she learned the property was being developed. "What's this neighborhood coming to?"

"It's probably just a rumor. Do you mind if I take some of these croissants back with me?"

My mother turned. "Of course not. I know how much you like them. That's why I bought so many."

I snagged one and stuffed a bite into my mouth. Here was a glimpse of the mother of my dreams, the one who thought about details and could show small kindnesses that always surprised me. "Thanks."

"So," she said with an encouraging smile, "are you going out with Steve tonight?"

I glanced at my father, who had settled at the kitchen table with a cup of coffee and the newspaper. He'd be reading the financial section, though we'd told him he could find better news online.

"No," I said. "Look, I've been wanting to talk to you guys. I've met someone. I'd like you to meet him tomorrow."

Silence fell, and for a long moment no one spoke. Even Tessa froze by the refrigerator, her eyes wide. My father lifted his gaze from the newspaper, his glasses on the end of his nose. "What's his name?"

"Mario Perez." I didn't know what made me use Mario, because Jameson would have been more appealing to them.

My mother's smile vanished. "Is that the man who was in your apartment?"

"Yes, but—"

"Oh, Lily," she said, folding her arms over her stomach in a pointed gesture. "This is your future, and your children's future. You have no idea what it is to manage a household or to pay for it. You need someone who can support you, who will be an asset to our family and your dad's company. You can't throw your life away on a sexy accent and hormones."

Accent? What was she talking about?

"Look, you go ahead and get this guy out of your system if you must," my father said. "But when you're ready to settle down, you need to make a choice you're not going to regret."

The only thing I regretted was coming home. Train wreck did not even begin to cover it. Or maybe the train analogy was a mistake because our train hadn't even gotten underway. Anyone could see that it didn't matter what I might say about Jameson or his family. Jameson's plan for the future and his love for me and my girls wouldn't change anything. My mother had made up her mind, and my father agreed with her.

"Are we clear?" my mother asked. At the table, my father had already gone back to his newspaper.

"Oh, we're clear." Just like that, her words freed me. Freed me from having to introduce them to Jameson, from seeking their blessing.

"Good. Now what shall we have for dinner?"

19

The house was dark and quiet. It was after one in the morning, and the alarm was on, but Tessa and I had long ago figured out how to bypass the sliding glass door leading to the second-floor balcony, which had stairs leading down to the lawn. We had carried several loads out to the front and were now waiting for Jameson. I'd texted him after the conversation with my parents, and he'd started driving the minute he'd dropped the girls off at the apartment after the fireworks were over in Phoenix.

Tessa leaned over to whisper. "I had no idea they'd be so . . . hard. They're never going to let you marry him."

"Well, fortunately, they don't have a say."

"What do you mean?"

"I mean, we're going to elope."

"Tonight?"

"Or tomorrow. Why not?"

Her mouth rounded to an O. "Are you absolutely sure? You've known him such a short time."

"Yeah, I'm sure. I can't explain how I know or how he makes me feel." How could she understand before she loved someone herself? "I love him so much. He's like the air that I breathe. We love the same things, we want to help people, and we don't care if our dishes and silverware match. We just want a house with love." A house without lies. "He's a hard worker, and I know we'll make it. You don't have to worry about me anymore."

Tessa hugged me. "Air that you breathe, huh? I hope someday I find someone who means that much to me."

"You will." At least she would if my parents didn't interfere.

"They do want the best for you," Tessa said, as if reading my mind.

"I know." The best in their view. "And Mom did buy me those croissants."

"Do you have them?"

"No. I don't think I can." I couldn't take anything like that from her, not now, not after the scene we'd had today.

She nodded. "Right."

My phone buzzed. "He's here."

"I should come with you. Someone from your family should be there when you get married."

I thought of the girls and Makay and knew I wouldn't be alone.

"I'll call you and let you know what we decide." I hugged her. "Goodbye! Lock up."

When I rounded the house, Jameson was packing my belongings into his car, but he stopped to hug me. The ice that had encased my heart all evening melted. This was right where I was supposed to be.

"That's some house," Jameson said, staring up at the

mansion. "I knew your family was well off, but I didn't expect this."

"Having second thoughts?"

"No. I love you. How could I ever have second thoughts?" Oh, his eyes were doing amazing things to my insides. "I may not be able to give you all this, but I promise to give you everything I have."

He already had. "Good, because I want to elope."

"Tonight?" He sounded like Tessa.

"Why not?"

"Okay. But can we tell my family first?"

Not exactly what I'd envisioned when I talked about eloping, but suddenly it was exactly right. "I'd like that."

"Good, because I don't know if my mother would forgive me if I didn't invite her."

"She would too."

"Yeah, but Angela wouldn't, and neither would our girls."

Our girls. I laughed. "You already convinced me."

"I'm glad. Hey, I have a surprise for you." He opened the car door and scooped up something from the seat. "The girls and I picked it out today." A velvet ring box sat in the middle of his palm. "It's just a band, but I swear I'll get you the biggest diamond you could ever want someday."

I kissed him. "I don't want one. I already have everything I want."

Thirty-two hours later on a brilliant Monday morning, Tessa stared out at me from a computer screen. "You look beautiful! I wish I could be there."

"You can't. I'm not coming between you and Mom and Dad." We both knew that if they ever found out she'd known about my elopement and not told them, she'd suffer. "That would make your work life miserable."

"I don't care about them."

I knew differently, but somehow I had to make her feel okay about this. "You don't understand, Tessa . . . you've been there for me all my life, whenever I needed you. You were mother and best friend. You kept my secrets and took care of me. Today isn't the end of everything. Just the beginning. So what if you're watching from a screen instead of holding my hand? I know you're with me in your heart. And you can be sure that after today, I'm still going to need you, and probably your money, so you have to keep your job. Besides, someday you're going to bring us all together. I know it."

She gave me a sad little smile. "You think they'll ever come around?"

"I don't know. Everyone changes. Now I have to go!" I handed the computer to Jameson's brother Tim, who had arranged for Tessa to virtually attend the ceremony.

Except for the suddenness, our attempt at elopement wasn't anything like eloping at all. We'd shown up at his parents' house yesterday, the girls and Makay with us, and this morning, Heidi had arranged for her local minister to perform the ceremony. Her friends had also organized a small celebration afterward, and Antonio and Jameson had somehow even come up with a two-night, three-day honeymoon on a Californian beach.

Heidi insisted that I wear her wedding dress, which was a little tight, but with a girdle Makay ran out to buy, I managed to squeeze into it. The simple sheath and modest train made my figure look amazing, but my favorite thing about the dress was the slight yellowing of the material.

Jameson wore a suit I didn't know he owned, and he looked so handsome and intelligent that I felt a moment of panic. Could he really love a woman like me? But the second he took my hand, all doubts vanished. It didn't matter where either of us came from, only how much we loved, what we dreamed, and how we worked for those dreams, no matter how impossible they seemed. I would be his light, and he would be my anchor, and together we'd build our future.

He leaned forward and whispered in my ear, "I love you."

I closed my eyes and breathed him in. He could always do that to me, make the world go away until there was just the two of us and no one else. This man, my heart, my soul, and keeper of my dreams. Wrapping my arms around his neck, I kissed him deeply. "I will always love you."

 EPILOGUE

I stood on the chair, stretching to screw in the curtain rod holder. It was the cheapest we could find, and rather ugly, but the curtains Michelle had made, not only for Elsie's room but for the entire house, covered the rods entirely.

Michelle had visited here often during the three months since we'd moved into the house, and though she wasn't ready yet to take responsibility for Elsie, the two had shared a few overnight stays at Michelle's. Both Michelle and her cousin had helped clean and paint the house, as well as make the curtains.

Outside, I glimpsed Jameson working in the yard by the front gate, my view of him partially obscured by a tree. He and I were both back in school, me with a new major in family sciences, and so far we were making it, but only because Makay, Tessa, and Saffron helped run the house. We still had the living room to paint, bare wood peeked through in the kitchen where pieces of linoleum were gone, and the yard was awful, but someday we'd get it all finished. Makay had planted a few flowers near the porch that made me happy every time I looked at them.

We'd added four girls to our family in the past month, but only one officially through DCS. The other three were runaways who'd shown up on our doorstep one day, all together, with a ragged scrap of the newspaper article someone had run about our efforts in refurbishing the house. After the article, someone had donated a green refrigerator, and a used washer and dryer were dumped off anonymously during the night. The new girls, however, were our best gift.

Ten girls and Makay and Nate meant we were already over capacity in our seven bedrooms, and I'd ended up clearing out the small office downstairs so Saffron could still have the private room I'd promised. We had a living room and a family room we could use for more girls in a pinch.

Or maybe in another year, a baby of our own.

The mailman was driving down the road, and Jameson went to meet the truck. Jameson accepted the handful of mail and scanned through the envelopes, freezing on one. His gaze shifted to the house, and our eyes locked through the window. He waved, but there was something odd in his expression. I jumped down from the chair and went to meet him.

He was faster than I was, joining me at the top of the stairs on the second floor. He handed me the envelope. "From your parents."

Trepidation filled me. I'd sent them pictures of the wedding and of the house, but they hadn't responded. I knew from Tessa that they were furious with me.

Slowly, I opened the envelope. Inside was the same article the runaways had carried here with them, but with it was a check. For ten thousand dollars.

I gasped and sat abruptly on the top stair. This must be a portion of the money they'd someday planned to spend on my wedding. Tessa had probably been working on them.

"What is it?" Jameson sat next to me.

"New tile for the kitchen," I said, trying to blink back tears. "Maybe enough for grass in the spring, and a walkway, if we do the kitchen tile ourselves." I let the check fall into his hands. We desperately needed the money, but what I really wanted was a letter, a phone call, a visit, or some indication that they had accepted my choices. That they understood the choices were mine to make.

Jameson wiped the tears on my cheeks, gazing into my eyes. "Sweetie, it's a start. It's their language, that's all. You should write to thank them." He hesitated. "Unless you want to send it back."

"No!" I'd accept for the girls. They needed so much, and Christmas was in less than two months. "You're right, and I will send them a thank-you card. But I think . . . instead of the grass, let's use some of it for bunkbeds in the bigger rooms. That way we can help—"

"More girls," he finished. Because the girls who weren't official foster children didn't count against our current joint eight child limit, so DCS might give us two more. "I guess grass can wait, and I've always wanted to learn how to tile."

He kissed me then, and my sadness vanished. My

parents would come around someday, maybe after Jameson and I proved ourselves. But I wasn't going to live my life wishing I could remake them. I'd made the right choices.

"Come on outside," Jameson said. "I have something to show you."

He took me down past the girls, who were watching a video in the living room, and outside to the gate. "I've been working on it in the garage for three weeks. Just got it up. How do you like it?"

He pointed to where he'd erected two elegantly carved wooden posts and a beautiful, handmade sign, white with carved letters painted in black that read *Lily's House.*

I laughed and threw myself into his arms, kissing him with abandon. "I love you Mario Jameson Perez."

"Not as much as I love you."

"Shut up and kiss me, would you?"

He did just that, stealing my breath and infusing me with delicious heat that radiated to every part of my body.

Lily's House.

Now I was definitely official.

Rachel Branton has worked in publishing for over twenty years. She loves writing women's fiction and traveling, and she hopes to write and travel a lot more. As a mother of seven, it's not easy to find time to write, but the semi-ordered chaos gives her a constant source of writing material. She's been known to wear pajamas all day when working on a deadline, and is often distracted enough to burn dinner. (Okay, pretty much 90% of the time.) A sign on her office door reads: Danger. Enter at Your Own Risk. Writer at Work. Under the name Rachel Branton, she writes romance, romantic suspense, and women's fiction. Rachel also writes urban fantasy, paranormal romance, and science fiction under the name Teyla Branton. For more information and to download a free Lily's House novella, please visit www.RachelBranton.com.